William Clark Russell

The Deceased Wife's Sister and my Beautiful Neighbour

Vol. 3

William Clark Russell

The Deceased Wife's Sister and my Beautiful Neighbour
Vol. 3

ISBN/EAN: 9783337416102

Printed in Europe, USA, Canada, Australia, Japan

Cover: Foto ©Andreas Hilbeck / pixelio.de

More available books at **www.hansebooks.com**

THE

DECEASED WIFE'S SISTER,

AND

MY BEAUTIFUL NEIGHBOUR.

IN THREE VOLUMES.

VOL. III.

LONDON: RICHARD BENTLEY & SON,
NEW BURLINGTON STREET.
1874.
The Right of Translation is reserved.

BEAUTIFUL NEIGHBOUR.

CHAPTER I.

I FOUND Martelli to be more useful to
me than I could have expected. He had
called himself practical, and he was practical.
He was used to the punctilious regularity
of schools, to the difficult inattention of
pupils; and the habits these experiences
had engendered well qualified him in one
sense for the post I had offered. In one
sense I say: by which I mean my need of
an influence to direct my studies and keep

me to them. But in him I missed what I had sought, and would have taken in preference, could I have found. Sympathies he had in abundance, but they were commonplace. He shone indeed ; but rather with the borrowed light of letters than the luminous atmosphere of imagination. He could not comprehend me, though he would never appear puzzled. He would miss a delicate implication. In taste he was a sensualist, esteeming the full-blooded, florid, and passionate conceptions of art above her chaste aerial hints and tender moonlit beauties. Yet he was a good and sound scholar. His knowledge of Greek and Latin was singularly exact. He was deeply read in modern literature ; and his surprising memory enabled him to display to the utmost advantage the various and carefully stored treasures of his mind. But though his erudition might have enabled him to have edited with accuracy the most obscure work in the whole range of ancient literature, his imagination would not have yielded him five lines of poetry.

When together in the library, he would often extort a smile from me by the recollection he excited of my school days. Brisk in his movements, energetic in his actions, pungent and austere in his resolute directions, he recalled to me a French tutor, whom, of all my early tutors, I most hated for his severity. But the task conned, the subject discussed, the book closed, his manner would change; he would be ceremoniously courteous, with almost a hint of obsequiousness in his behaviour, as though he wished me to understand that his sturdy discharge of his duty did not prevent him from appreciating the difference of position between us.

I should have benefited more from his counsels had my thoughts been less preoccupied with the subject which was hardly ever absent from my mind.

But I found it impossible wholly to surrender my attention to my tasks. Memory persistently reverted to the strange and beautiful apparition that had startled me in my midnight saunter. Every day, nay, every hour, was increasing my desire to know her. Yet I could hit upon no means of introduction. To have hung about her house, to have loitered near her garden, even had the absence of my companion rendered such a device practicable, would have been unwise; since, if now from no apparent cause she shunned intrusion or inspection, greater would be her efforts to maintain her privacy when she discovered a stranger sought to violate it.

One thing I could not hide from myself— I was in love with her. I am well aware that under the circumstances the feeling was most absurd; but I could not help it. The memory of her beauty took shape before me at all hours, in all moods. And my love was illustrated and confirmed by my wish to meet, to know, to speak with her.

Martelli noticed my abstraction. More than once I had remarked his dusky eyes glowing on me with a gaze of interrogative inspection. But he carefully repressed his curiosity. No observation ever escaped him to hint his perception of inattentive moods.

Once, meeting his eyes, it occurred to me to take him into my confidence.

" The Italians," I mused, "are famous for their handling of love matters. They at least bear the reputation of being subtle and secret in such adventures. They wind into the most tortuous intrigues like a snake through the intricacies of a forest. Why not tell him my story? A young man in love with a woman whom he has seen but once, is an object neither remarkable nor unique. He might aid me by procuring an introduction, at all events; and if he can do this, he has my full consent to think what he likes of the business."

It was evening. We were seated at a table in the library, near the window, which was wide open to admit the still and sultry air. There was no moon; but the stars, large, full and liquid, lent a pale radiance to the gloom. I rose, took a cigar from the mantel-piece and lighted it.

"Let us close these books for to-night," I said. "The air is oppressive; and those sweet stars seem to chide us for preferring the inspiration of other things to theirs."

He smiled, drew a meerschaum from his pocket, and began to smoke. I pushed the table aside that I might seat myself more fully in the window.

" There is a line in one of Keats's poems—
' Hyperion,' " I said.

"I know it," he interrupted. " A noble
poem."

" Noble, indeed. There is a line in that
poem which I do not think I ever
thoroughly understood until now. I refer
to the line in which he speaks
of

—' tall oaks, branch-charmed by the earnest stars.'

Look at those round, moony orbs, tremulous
like tears wept by the gods ; the trees yonder
seem spell-bound beneath them."

" Truly," he answered.

" Surely theirs is a magical repose: a
deeper calm than that of sleep. Oh, I can
forgive much to the superstition of astrology.
Those planets deserve to be influences if
they are not. The malignant heart would
of course make their shine sinister ; but a
generous nature must deem those clear rays

benignant. I do. But it is the common effect of Beauty on me. I warm, I dilate in her presence. She is a glorious spirit."

"Ay, to a man of taste."

"Beauty of course is a spirit inter-penetrating all that delights and elevates. But she is incarnate too, sometimes; falling, I suppose, from the heavens like that meteor there," I said, pointing to an exhalation that rushed with yellow tresses streaming through the dark ; "and taking the shape of a woman when she touches the earth."

"But is not innocence a condition of beauty?" he inquired, turning his dusky gaze upon me.

"It should be."

"Then do not make your spirit take the shape of woman."

I laughed. "What shape would you have her?"

He shrugged his shoulders. "I hardly know," he answered: "unless you make her a new-born babe."

"I fear you have the scholar's contempt for the *tendre passion*," said I. "But listen now to a strange story. Do you see those trees yonder?"

"Yes, Sir."

"One night—it was clear with moonlight—I strolled out to breathe the air. My excursion extended to those fields you can see from your bedroom window. There I lingered. The village clock struck two. Hardly had the silvery notes died, when——"

I paused.

"You returned home, Sir?"

"No. But looking, I perceived the Spirit of Beauty walking beneath the starlight, draped in white, with eyes deep and beautiful, in which the moon hid itself for love, with a face of marble, passionless as the feature of the mother of Paphus ere the sculptor's adoration made her rosy with life."

He showed his gleaming teeth in a smile of which he thought the gloom would hide the contempt.

"Sir," he said, -"you are talking the language of the romancist."

"I am talking the language of truth."

"At two o'clock in the morning," he exclaimed, blowing a white cloud on the air, "the female shapes one meets abroad are seldom spiritual. How they may look in the country, and by starlight, I do not know; but by gaslight their cadaverous complexion is commonly cloaked with paint; and if their eyes are bright, it is rather with a spirituous than a spiritual ray."

"Ah, Martelli, you are a cynic—by which I mean, a practical, astute man, who makes the root and not the flower of fact or fancy his business. A commendable quality! All

the same, I would not part with my love of
illusion. This essential difference of character will make us get on well together;
though, to be plain, before I knew you, my
opinion was that if I hoped to please or be
pleased, my comrade must be a man of sympathies identical with my own."

"A common and generous error," he replied ; "but time corrects those crudities."

"As a proof, I like you none the worse
for the misanthropic pleasure you take in
extinguishing the candle in the magic-lantern
of fancy—at the moment when the panoramic
reflections most delight me. But respecting
this apparition—here is no illusion ; for I
have found out who she is."

He smoked in silence.

" Her name is Mrs. Fraser. She is a widow.
She lives in that house yonder, where the
light shines through the trees. I have only
seen her once, and the circumstances of that
meeting may have served to exaggerate my

impression of her. But the recollection I
carried away with me is that of a woman of
a beauty whose mysteriousness defies descrip-
tion."

"If you desire to be disenchanted, Mr.
Thorburn, you should get to know her."

"I should be happy to risk my idealism ;
but how am I to procure an introduction ?
Her house is a cloister—she a nun, secret
and exclusive as the austerest of the flannelled
sisterhood."

"Were we in Italy, I should advise you
to serenade her. There love is studied as
a fine art. It is different here. Yet were I
in your straits—for, Mr. Thorburn, are
you not in love with this beautiful phantom
of yours?"

"I confess it."

"If I were in your straits, I say, I should
do something hardy ; go to her home,
procure admittance at any sacrifice of politeness, and leave the rest to chance."

"That would be practicable to a man with a temperate pulse and trained nerves," I replied; "but I believe I could much more easily jump off the cliff than place myself in the position you suggest."

"But you say you met her, Sir. Did she not see you?"

"No. She stood some yards from me tranquil and statuesque, quite unconscious of my presence—*that* I could swear."

"Surely she must have seen you—the moon, you said, was bright."

"She did *not* see me. It is true I uttered an exclamation of surprise when I found her so close to me; for I thought she had vanished. She may have heard that cry."

"But what should this lady be doing in the fields at two o'clock in the morning?" he asked, with a light smile.

"That is precisely what I wish to know."

He slowly filled another pipe, with his lips moving as though in the process of rehearsal.

" Mr. Thorburn," said he, " I am sure you will excuse my freedom. I really think you should banish this subject from your mind. You have settled here for the purpose of prosecuting a good and lofty purpose, and you should suffer nothing to seduce you from devoting your whole energies to its accomplishment. No man can serve two mistresses. And knowledge, Sir, let me assure you, is a mistress who, if she does not receive your whole heart, will give you little in return."

" Your candour requires no apology, Martelli," I answered. " I am sure you speak for my good, and I am grateful for the interest you take in me. But I must tell you that this woman has occupied my thoughts so long, that it is become a positive necessity to know her. Don't smile at what

I am about to say—I protest, for my part,
I was never more in earnest—I believe," I
said solemnly, " that this woman is to be an
influence on my life—though whether bane-
ful or benignant is still the secret of the
future. Why do you shrug your shoulders?
Don't you believe in presentiments—in the
power of the soul to foreshadow destiny?
A few hours before I met her—this lady—
she presented herself to me in a dream.
Your sceptical mind would pronounce this
a coincidence—the very dream, you think,
might have generated the subsequent vision.
But it was no coincidence. It was the
operation of some mystic agency, to be
credited without questioning; an agency as
definite, though inscrutable, as the soul
which informs our being with the knowledge
of its existence, but ridicules our efforts to
give that knowledge shape."

" Have you ever sought to meet her
again?"

"I have not dared."

"Not *dared !*"

"You are surprised. But I had not Hamlet's resolution :

> " ' Be thou a spirit of health or goblin damn'd,
>   Bring with thee airs from heaven or blasts from hell,
>   Be thy intents wicked or charitable,
>   Thou comest in such questionable shape,
>   I *dare not* speak to thee !'

Martelli, had I met her close again, as I met her that night, I should have gone mad. Her steady supernatural gaze, her rigid mien, her shape, which united the two extremes of spectral beauty and human sweetness, were shocking."

"Would you fear to meet her if you had a companion."

"I hardly know. Pray applaud my candour ; you see I confess myself a coward."

"It is no proof of cowardice. A brave man might reasonably recoil from encountering such an airy horror as enlivened your midnight ramble. As for me, I have no fear of ghost or goblin. A questionable shape would make me curious, not timid. Here, however, we should be dealing with no shadow. . A phantom might, indeed, be a widow, though, it is said, that owing to the scarcity of priests, there are no marriages in Heaven. But it would hardly bear the name of ' Mrs. Fraser,' when it has a magnificent mythology to choose from. At what time did you say you met her ?"

" It was two o'clock in the morning."

" A rather inconvenient hour," he exclaimed with a laugh. " Would not ten or eleven o'clock suit her as well? But it is enough that she should be a woman to be perverse. If you think that there is any chance of our meeting her to-night, I should be glad to accompany you. Two heads are better than one in a business of this kind."

" I am willing to go. Yet there is no reason why she should be there."

"We shall have the moon with us, at all
events," he said ; "for there she is, crawling
up yonder, though with a sinister disc."

He pointed to the trees, above which the
moon, large, red, and dim, like a cloud
shone on by the expiring sun, was slowly
sailing up.

"It is now half-past ten," I remarked.
"It may prove after all a fool's errand.
However we can sip our grog and stroll
out afterwards, if you like—go, at all events,
to the fields, and linger in the cool till you
shall think proper to return."

He consented, though assuring me it
would be no inconvenience to him to sit
through the night.   He was anxious, he
added, that I should have my mind cleared
of the odd fancies that encumbered it; and
very proud and happy would it make him
to believe that he had been instrumental in
solving any problem that perplexed, or
helping forward any desires that agitated me.

I did not doubt, though he was cautious not to suggest, that he thought me a very odd, fanciful, even half-crazy being. A downright practical intrigue, a transparent love-affair, he could very readily have understood; but a passion excited by meeting a woman under circumstances so strange, a love inflamed by superstition and yet made imbecile by timidity, it was not in his nature to comprehend. It was fortunate perhaps that his polite incredulity curbed my natural tendency to rhapsodise, or I might have written myself down a greater ass in his eyes than he was disposed to think me.

We left the house at an hour considerably past the appointed time. Sitting over our brandy-and-water we had fallen into an argument, and had prosecuted it with an industry and enthusiasm that had made us forgetful of the clock. He was the first to recall our scheme.

"See!" he exclaimed, "it is twenty minutes to twelve; close upon the hour when churchyards yawn."

"Come, then," said I; "but lest we encounter more than our nerves—*my* nerves at all events—are prepared to meet, let us take one glass more."

He refused with a smile. I brimmed a tumbler.

"*Ai mali extremi, extremi remedi,*" said he, laughing.

"You may need the remedy yourself yet," I retorted, as I led the way into the garden.

The air was so silent that, as we marched with soundless tread upon the velvet lawn, I could hear the rustle of an occasional leaf falling from the branches. Among the trees the moon threw level beams, that lay like fallen marble columns. The shadows were swart and stirless.

I was kept silent by my thoughts. He

was loquacious. We gained the end of the grounds, passed through the gate, and entered the fields.

"What an oppressive night!" he exclaimed, removing his hat and fanning himself with it. "The moon seems hardly able to pierce her light through the sultry air. I should have thought such a temperature impossible in fifty-five degrees north."

"It must end in a storm. The stars look white and sick with the heat. Perhaps they are paling their ineffectual fires before the brilliance of the lightning which they can see but we cannot."

We had gained the summit of the hillock whereon I had before stood. I seated myself.

"There is her house, or rather there is its position," said I, pointing to the trees. "Do you see that hedge? She was gliding alongside it when I saw her. Martelli, picture yourself alone here; disposed by the drowsy moonlight and vague murmurs in the air to unpleasant thoughts. Suddenly a white dim shape flits upon the gloom, pauses, vanishes, to reappear at your elbow—would you not use your legs?"

His white teeth shone beneath his black moustache.

"No. It would probably be the other who would use its legs. I should seize it— man or woman, angel or goblin!"

"Then your nerves must be of galvanised wire, your muscles iron, your spirit something more surprising than the timid essence that vitalises such a lower order of being as I."

He smoked the cheroot I had given him, without response.

I lay back with my head reposing on my arm, my eyes fixed on the stars.

"Look!" he suddenly cried; "there is your spirit!"

I started—rose to my feet at once. She

stood, habited as I had before seen her, at the gate of the garden, motionless.

Martelli advanced, paused, beckoned. I went to him.

"Shall we go to her?" he whispered. "If she sees us she will withdraw."

"She will not see us."

He laughed low.

"She must be blind if she doesn't. But now is your opportunity to speak with her. Come with me—be bold, Sir. This is a rare chance. Should she not see us until we are near, and then attempt to withdraw, accost her bravely. Tell her you have met her here before — acquaint her with your alarm. The rest is easy."

He moved forward; I followed. The moon gave us sharp, short shadows. I breathed quickly. He heard my pantings, and took my arm.

She stood confronting us; but she did not stir. We drew near. I who knew her face, could shape from the countenance, whose lineaments were yet too dim to discern, the sorrowful sovereign eyes and immobile beauty.

Suddenly Martelli stopped short. I looked at him. He was staring and trembling. His breath seemed to die. His eyes were round and lively with an expression that seemed to me akin to horror. I heard him gasp "*Dio mio! Dio mio!*" several times.

Somehow the failure of his courage was the renewal of mine. Much of her mystery had at least fallen from this woman. I knew who she was, at all events. But how strange, how startling was it to see her gazing steadfastly in our direction, and not offering to move.

I whispered to Martelli: "Come, come! where are your nerves?" He could not answer me. There he stood, rooted to the ground, with his face in the moonlight blanched to the colour of a corpse.

At this moment the figure turned, made a gesture with her right hand and withdrew.

"I will follow you!" I said, setting my teeth, for the undertaking was a mighty one to me. Yes! I was mastered now by a resolution uncontrollable as superstition and passion could make it, to speak to her. I left Martelli and advanced to the gate. I pushed it open, and passed up the garden walk. Her white shape floated in front. I trod on tiptoe, gained her side, and whispered :

"I saw your summons. I am, indeed, grateful to you for this privilege. I have long wished for an interview, but respected too much your obvious desire of solitude "——

But here I broke off; for though I spoke in her ear she did not turn. Had she been a statue, she could not have been more heedless. I was abreast of her; a stride took me in advance. I looked into her face. Her eyes were fixed. In their wonderful depth the moon was mirrored; but they were uninformed and expressionless. They stared from beneath her brow of ivory, soulless and blank.

I halted abruptly, as Martelli had done. She swept forward, mounted the steps leading into the house, and vanished. I returned to my friend. I found him leaning against the gate. When he saw me he stood erect. His face was still blanched; but he had mastered himself so far as to speak in a firm voice and to smile.

" She is no ghost," he said briefly.

" I knew that," I replied.

" She was very ghostly though. I can understand your alarm."

" I am glad you can. Your own behaviour justifies mine. But I thought you were afraid of neither ghost nor goblin ?"

" I thought she would move—I thought

she would move," he replied. "Her stillness was fearful—it was unexpected—I found
it terrible."

"But the mystery of her is at an
end."

"I know what you mean, Sir. Your
ghost is nothing more than a somnambulist.
I should have guessed it from the beginning
—guessed either that she was asleep or that
she was mad. Anyone in his senses would
have hit upon this."

"I didn't. But perhaps I am not in my
senses."

"Remember, Sir, you are in love!" he
exclaimed, with a hard laugh.

"Who could help being in love with
such a creature? Did you remark her
beauty?"

"As well as I could by the light. She
did not strike me as possessing the charms
your enthusiasm would have suggested. To
be sure I saw her at a disadvantage. But I

do not admire red-haired women ; or if they be red-haired, let them have at least blue eyes. Beauty should always be harmonious. And then she walks in her sleep—a qualification I for one could dispense with."

"Let us go in," I said. "The issue of this adventure has satisfied me. To-morrow I will introduce myself to her."

CHAPTER II.

THE resolution I had made over night was stronger by the morning. When I met Martelli I told him there would be no use in sitting down to work.

" I foresaw this," he replied. " Perhaps it will be better to defer your studies until you are out of this mysterious complication," smiling.

" It will hardly be optional," I said. " My mind is too active in a very different direction from books to make me profit from reading. The labour would only be mechanical."

" I wish, Sir, you would direct me to

employ the interval in some way useful to
yourself. I shall be eating the bread of
idleness—a food I have little relish
for."

"You will be doing nothing of the sort,"
I answered ; "your society gives me pleasure, and besides, we may take a holiday
now and then, may we not? We have
done very well. In the time you have
been here, you have advanced me further
than I could have done alone in twelve
months."

He bowed, thanking me for my assurance,
and expressed his gratitude for the unfailing
politeness and liberal hospitality he had
enjoyed during his residence.

He had recovered from his surprise or
shock of the preceding night. Yet there
was upon his manners and in his expression
a shadow whose presence I could mark,
though whose meaning I could not read.
The subtle alteration would, have been

inappreciable to one who had watched him less closely than I, and who had been less often in his company. There was a light now in his eye which had not been there before. His energy, the swift gesture, the sharp vanishing smile, the quick contraction of the brow, were moderated, sobered, by a stealthy composure. I attributed the change, vague and slight as it was, to the fright he had received. "This hint of unfamiliar repose," I said to myself, "may be the effect of repressed ˙irritability, excited by his last night's involuntary confession of weakness or cowardice."

I had a part to play, however, which gave my thoughts full employment.

I left Martelli and strolled about the grounds until lunch-time. I then returned, despatched a light meal, took my hat, and left the house. Elmore Cottage was not above five minutes' walk from my house by the road. I could have wished it ten

times the distance. I approached it timor-
ously, and gazed bashfully under the con-
cealment of the hedge. It was an exquisitely
clean little place: the walls white, the
windows burnished and draped with snowy
muslin. The lower windows were veiled
with flowers. I hoped its mistress would
not see me enter. I rather prayed that
she might be in the garden. I pushed
open the gate with a quick hand and gained
the door. My thin and doubtful appeal
with the knocker was promptly answered
by a young woman, tidy, grave, and
comely.

I asked for Mrs. Fraser. I was answered
that she was out.

"She will not be out to me," said I,
"if you will say that I am come to speak
with her on a matter of great consequence
to herself."

The servant eyed me shrewdly, though

not disrespectfully. "But Mrs. Fraser is out, Sir," said she.

"Mrs. Fraser is not out," I exclaimed in a steady voice. "Come, allow me to walk in. Must I repeat that I have come to see Mrs. Fraser on very important business?"

She was too well-trained to keep me on the doorstep or even in the passage, though I daresay she would have preferred that I remained in the road whilst she went to hold a council with her mistress. She slightly smiled as she said, "What name, Sir?"

"Never mind my name," I replied. "Simply say a gentleman has called to see her."

She left the room. The apartment into which she had conducted me was close, though the windows were open. The furniture was old, but tasteful enough. A piano stood in a corner, and on a chair was a pile of music. I thought of my bouquet as my eye rested on some flowers in a vase on the table. On either side the mirror, over the chimney-piece, was a pencil drawing, skilfully done, representing, the one on the left, a calm at sea, an iceberg on the horizon, an albatross suspended over the wreck of a vessel, whose broken masts, trailing ropes and vacant decks were full of the poetry of desolation: the one on the right, a woman seated at a table, with her face buried in her hands, a crucifix before her. I drew near, and read at the corner of each drawing the word " Geraldine."

A longer interval than what I had antici-pated elapsed before Mrs. Fraser presented herself. I was eyeing a little gilt dial with some degree of impatience, when I heard a sound behind me. I turned rapidly.

Mrs. Fraser stood at the table, her black eyes fixed on me with a look half of alarm, half of embarrassment. Their startled beauty was smiting. Her yellow hair was combed high, but silken threads strayed over her brow and behind her ears. Her lips were compressed.

I rose and made her a bow.

" Pray be seated," she said in a low voice. " My servant tells me you have called on a matter of business."

" Not exactly *business*," I answered. " But first, you must allow me to introduce myself to you as Mr. Thorburn, your neighbour."

She regarded me earnestly. I paused : another moment's silence would have embarrassed me, so I said hardily :

" I shall wholly depend on your kindness not to make me feel more painfully the trying position in which I have placed myself. The intrusion," continued I, nervousness making my apology elaborate, " will only seem all the more unwarrantable when I tell you that I am fully aware of

your love of solitude and your aversion to
intruders. But "——

She interrupted me, turning her back to
the window, the better to see me, and not
to be seen :

"You sent me a bouquet the other
day ?"

"I ventured to take the liberty."

"You must have thought my rejection
rude. It was meant to be rude. How, Sir,
knowing my aversion to intruders, *could*
you have taken that liberty ? Did you
think it would lead to an introduction ?"

Her language gave me confidence. Had
she sweetly thanked me for my attention or
apologised for her rudeness, she would, I
think, have confounded me too much for
my wits. But this tone of hers brought her
down to my level. I could meet her on
equal ground.

"I sent you that bouquet," I answered,
"because I judged by your love of garden-

ing that you were fond of flowers. The action was not designed as a rudeness. It was a mere neighbourly act "——

She seemed too impatient to hear me out.

" How can I believe you? People never act without design."

"I have explained my design," I said, repressing a smile with difficulty.

Her eyes were incensed. Their beauty made them almost unreal.

" You are still standing!" she exclaimed. "I beg that you will be seated. Pray do not mind me. I am of an excitable temperament, and when I converse it is difficult for me to keep still."

She left the window, went to the end of the room, and gazed at me thence, like some beautiful savage, untamed, startled, exquisitely unconventional.

I borrowed her tone; she was freespoken; she would like free-speaking.

"My apology—if apology it were—does not contain the whole truth. But your goodness will not allow you to think me so great a culprit as I appear. I had met you once; your appearance piqued me; I desired to make your acquaintance and have tried an experiment which I beseech you not to render ignominious."

"Piqued, Sir! How were you piqued?"

"Piqued is not the word. But I dare not substitute the right expression. I will not be so rude as to utilise the privilege your own candour confers."

She came over and stood opposite me.

"You say, Mr. Thorburn, you have met me. That is impossible."

"If I prevaricated before, I am truthful now."

"I have not been out of this house for a month. Oh! I suppose you saw me from your grounds."

"The thick hedge and the trees that divide us would prevent that."

"You may have found the means of looking over?"

I smiled.

"No, indeed. Great as my curiosity may have been, my politeness, I am sure, is vigorous enough to keep it well disciplined."

"Curiosity! what should there be in me to excite curiosity?"

"Curiosity is the daughter of admiration."

"I am a widow," she continued vehemently. "I lead a sequestered life. I visit nowhere. I receive no visits. Is it because I am a Roman Catholic that you are curious?"

"Do you take me for a missionary, Mrs. Fraser? I assure you I was ignorant of your faith. Of your habits I know only from the information of my housekeeper. A fellow-feeling makes us kind. I, too, am a recluse, loving solitude as well as yourself."

"Impossible!" she exclaimed impetuously, "or you would not have called here."

I could have told her that I loved beauty more than solitude. But I held my tongue.

"Where did you meet me?" she asked.

"I met you in the fields outside our respective grounds."

"Never!" she cried. "Never have I passed the gate that leads into those fields."

There was something singular in her vehemence. But it made her beauty more remarkable by the life it imparted to it.

"But this has been told me before," she continued rapidly. "Yes, I remember. Your housekeeper asked my servant if I were not in the habit of taking midnight rambles. Oh, how can you justify the rudeness of such questions?"

"They were asked unknown to myself. Be sure, I should never have sanctioned them. If I had questions to ask, I should be bold, and interrogate you, not your domestic."

" Questions to ask! What are you to me that you should question me?"

" Nothing. I am to you no more than your servant is to me. But you are something to me. Is it possible, do you think, that I could look upon your face without interest?"

" How should I know—why should I care?" she replied, her nostrils dilated, her lips curved, her eyes radiant with the light of anger qualified by surprise—of resentment tempered by curiosity. " You say you met me—you are long in telling your story."

" It was one moonlight night. I walked to the fields, and had seated myself, when I saw you pacing the walk by the hedge. Twice you went the length of it—then disappeared."

She seated herself in a chair facing mine, leaned her chin upon her small white hand,

and gazed at me with a look of earnestness that was embarrassing in its intensity. The pressure upon her chin made her speak through her teeth as she said,

"You must have dreamed this?"

"Indeed I did not. But I own I dreamt of you before. I dreamt that you looked upon me in a vision. I saw your eyes. They were not more wonderful in that vision than they are in life. Your face was paler than it is now."

She did not alter her position.

"A few hours after this dream I saw you. The spirit I had seen in my sleep stood before me in the flesh. This singular realisation of my vision made a deep impression. Its natural consequence was a great eagerness to know you. But how could I intrude? under what pretext could I force myself upon you? Last night I found an excuse—I met you again."

"How strange!" she muttered. She had

dropped her forehead upon her hand and her deep eyes shone upon me through their long lashes.

" When I met you last night," I continued, " I was not alone. A companion was with me. You appeared to us as you had appeared to me. He saw you, and if you doubt the truth of what I say, will bear testimony. You stood at the gate ; your eyes were fixed and your countenance turned towards us."

A look of distress entered her face.

" I did not know that I still walked in my sleep," she said.

" It is a dangerous habit, Mrs. Fraser."

" I will give directions to my servant. I am grateful to you *now* for your visit. I see you did not design to do me a rudeness. I should have received you more courteously ; but I am not always my own mistress."

" Indeed ?" I answered ; " your candour is too charming to require excuses. You must believe that such ingenuousness is very refreshing to one who, like myself, has wasted the best part of his days amid sophisticated and conventional society, where truth is never possible because it must always be offensive."

"Don't you find it dull at Elmore Court?"

"No; I spend the greater portion of my time in reading. Besides, I have a companion—a gentleman accomplished enough to be of great use to me in my studies."

"You are a young man," she said, eyeing me intently, "and it is unusual for young men to banish themselves from life and its pleasures, especially if they have money."

"I admire your incredulity," I answered, laughing, "for it gives me an excuse to tell you more of myself than I could otherwise have done. I mean, that a voluntary confession would have smacked rather egotistic."

She left her chair and began to pace up and down the room. I was fascinated by her form, the beautiful curve of her breast, the proportioned waist, her erect stature, and the unconscious grace of her movements. When her face was towards me her eyes were invariably on mine ; there was in them an unsmiling sparkle, a grave glow, that gave unreality to their gaze, a spectral beauty to their depths.

" I took Elmore Court," I continued, " not because I was tired of, but because I wanted to enjoy, life."

" You thought that abstinence would create appetite ?"

" I wished to learn the art of living ; and this, I saw, was only to be accomplished by study, by thought, and by awakening aspirations which should be lofty enough to make their achievement laborious."

" What do you hope to do ?"

" Much."

" You will do little. Ah! you think I mean that you have no talent? I have not

said so. How should I know your gifts
and deficiencies? But life itself is one huge
disappointment. The more laborious the
effort the more dreadful the failure. Pray
don't fancy I think only of books, or art,
or science. I know nothing of these things;
and they make but a very small portion of
life. I have the passions in my mind—love,
hope, patience and the like—all these things
end in regret."

" Your logic is very dispiriting," said I,
watching her with increasing admiration.
" It would leave life nerveless, and make
death its only aspiration."

" Do you think life ends in death?"

" The life of the flesh, certainly."

" The flesh has nothing to do with life.
It is the spirit that lives. My flesh might
have been dead last night when you saw
me: for I heard and felt nothing. No!
it was all as blank to me as my sight when I
shut my eyes so ;" she closed her eyes like a

child would have done. "I might have been dead, and to myself was as dead as ever I shall be when I am in the grave."

I was about to speak, when she suddenly said, " Mr. Thorburn, you are making a long call."

" I must plead you as my excuse," I answered, rising, hardly knowing whether to look grave or smile, so bewildered was I by her manners and conversation : her brusquerie, of which her beauty qualified the rudeness ; her severity, tempered by a childishness which made all her moods but new points of view of her charms.

I took my hat : she opened the door.

" I hope, Mrs. Fraser," said I, " that you will not deny me the pleasure of meeting you again ?"

" I have not come to Cliffegate for society, Mr. Thorburn."

" Nor I. But a single individual does not

make society.   Besides, would not my having
met you twice under circumstances so un-
common justify my claiming a privilege
to which no one else in this place could
pretend ?"

"What privilege ?"

"The privilege of knowing you and meeting you.   It was, at least, promised me in
a dream.   You will not set aside a promise
so mysterious?"

"Are you a fatalist?   I am.   If you are
not, you will ridicule my *weakness*, as you
will call it.   But much may be forgiven to
persons who lead such self-contained lives as
I.   So, if we are to become friends, our
friendship is preordained, and my rebelling
against it would be foolish."

"If we are to be friends, I shall become
a fatalist.   A creed made tempting by such
a reward is irresistible.   I have your per-
mission to call again ?"

"You are your own master."

The reply was sufficient. I extended my hand ; she gave me hers. I held it for a moment, and we separated.

CHAPTER III.

MARTELLI was in the library when I entered. He sat deep in an arm-chair, his legs crossed, his face hid behind a folio.

"I have seen my apparition," said I cheerfully.

"I guessed so by the time you were absent," he answered, looking at the clock.

"I hope my resolute behaviour vindicates my courage, or at least excuses my former fears."

"You have renewed the pretty ancient legend, and have changed your shape of marble into a breathing woman. It certainly shows some hardihood and much tact to have penetrated into her presence. She seems, by your account, to have taken the white veil of solitude, and is dead to all the world."

"After an interview with a beautiful woman," I cried effusively, looking round upon the bookshelves, "how flat, stale, weary, and unprofitable appears everything else! The dead are all very well in their way—*nil nisi bonum*—but there is something in the large black eye of a woman—a divinity, a power, an inspiration—that makes poetry, philosophy and the fine arts very second-rate, somehow."

"No, Sir; the rate is not changed; it is a only temporary eclipse—a shadow dimming a light."

"Well," said I, "for my part, I adore black eyes; I refer particularly to Mrs. Fraser's. If I were called upon to name the most harmonious contrast in the world,

I should say black eyes and yellow hair.
Oh! she is the loveliest, the most fascinating,
the wildest, sweetest, strangest woman in
the wide world!"

"Your interview has been satisfactory, I
presume?" he remarked drily. "She must
have been prepared for your visit and met
you with the most polished and facile of her
arts."

"There was nothing polished or facile
about her. On the contrary, she was
rude."

"Indeed!"

"Yes—what would be called rude were I
to write it down. But you know I am a
bit of a gourmand and relish pungent condi-
ments. Her manner is indeed the only
sauce piquante that would suit her beauty."

"'We forgive in proportion as we love,'
says Rochefoucauld, a man of the world."

"There is nothing to forgive—but there
is much to love. There is a shrewd sweet-

ness about her that took me mightily. Solitude has made her primitive. Had Byron met her we should have had a poem on the beautiful savage, with her coy and mutinous manners, with the light of golden sands upon her hair and the shine of torrid suns upon her eyes. Hear me now, Martelli, and marvel!" I continued, striking a heroic attitude. "When she speaks she looks like liberty incarnate ; there is freedom in her royal gestures; pliancy and power in her step; her exquisite form undulates to her thoughts like the shadow of a dryad seen in a breezy pool!"

"This, Sir, is love. Your language has about it the poetic ambiguity that no other passion would dictate."

"It is love! I avow it. I am in love with this woman."

"I think I can understand you, Sir. You have cultivated this emotion for the purpose of utilising it. You are giving it full licence that you may properly observe its operation. When fully developed, you will anatomise it, study its conformation, and having enlarged your knowledge of human nature by the examination, bury the corpse of the passion as the doctors bury the subjects they have dissected."

" No, this is not my intention," I answered, laughing heartily; "emotion is too valuable to be wasted in the pursuit of knowledge."

" Pardon me, Sir, but—do you propose to marry her?"

" If she will have me."

"She is to be congratulated on her beauty. It must be of a rare and powerful kind to strike love at one blow into a heart which I thought was surfeited with this sort of thing."

" Her beauty is rare and powerful too."

" It must be, to achieve such a victory

over the experience that had driven you
into the cool and calm dominion of intellectual love."

"Can I not occupy both dominions?
Must intellect be denied me because I
fall in love?" I asked, attributing the sar-
castic emphasis of his language to a fear
that my marriage would lose him his
situation.

"I think not," he answered. "My experience of knowledge is, that it is a jealous
god. Surely, Sir, your resolution is abrupt!
You have declared your intention only to
excite my wonder!"

"On the contrary, I am quite sincere
when I tell you that I am head over heels
in love with this woman, and that I would
marry her to-morrow if I thought she would
accept me."

He rose, went to the window, stared out
for some moments, and then approached
me.

"If I understood you aright, Mr. Thorburn, your object in residing here was to enable you to lay in such a stock of knowledge as would enable you to contest for fame with a good promise of success?"

I nodded.

"You even went, Sir, to the expense of furnishing this house, that you might burden yourself with obligations which should not be got rid of without inconvenience and loss."

"True."

"That you did, that your resolution, should it grow impaired by fatigue or caprice, would still be hampered with difficulties enough to make its decay slow or even impossible."

"Well?" said I, wondering at his solemnity and long preamble.

"Is it possible, Sir, I ask respectfully, that you will abandon your large and dignified enterprise for a lady of whom you know nothing?"

"You only make me sensible of the capriciousness of my character," I answered, laughing ; " but you could not shake the love this lady has inspired."

" Sir," he said courteously, " nothing would justify the freedom of my language but the knowledge that one of the duties you desired me to discharge, was to stimulate your energies when I found them flagging. But as you have determined to alter your views, I shall of course consider those duties at an end."

" Why ?" I asked. " What avenues in life would be closed to me as a married man that are opened to me as a bachelor? A man is not bound to be idle, is not pro-hibited from meditating as ambitiously as he chooses, because he gives his name to a woman."

" I do not say, Sir, that you may not recur hereafter to your schemes ; but you may reckon on being very indisposed for study for a good time now. This lady will occupy your thoughts to the exclusion of all things else, before marriage and for long after. Love-making is an absorbing occupation. To a poor man it may be a stimulus, for he may have to work in order to wed; but to a rich man it is usually a soporific."

"My good friend," I exclaimed, "you speak as though my marriage were a fixed matter. Let us look at the truth. I am in love with this lady, it is true—but she is not in love with me. I may have to be importunate to procure her consent—should she ever vouchsafe her consent, which, between you and me, I have no earthly reason to suppose likely; and importunities, to be successful, must be often delayed and never vehement. I should regret your leaving me; and should regret it the more if you resolve to go before my future takes a more definite character. My wishes will

of course impel me to bring this love of
mine to an issue as speedily as she will let
me ; but I really like your company too
well to wish you to regulate your conduct by a contingency which, I fear, may
prove the reverse of inevitable."

He paced the room, eyeing me from
time to time with a gaze uncertain and
agitated. His brow was clouded.

"I am very grateful to you for your
kindness to me," he said, "and I will avail
myself of it to think a little before I decide.
I shall be selfish enough to hope that your
marriage will not happen. We have been
going on well—very well. It would be
a pity that this pleasant life should be disturbed. I am much obliged to you for
your courtesy," he repeated, "and you are
very kind to have listened to my plain-
speaking so good-naturedly."

To this I made some reply, and the
subject dropped.

" Here," thought I, " is an illustration
of the genuine southern character : the warm
and sudden humours ; the irritable pets and
fumes ; the querulous misgivings ; the effu-
sive gratitude ; the morbid distrust. Here
too, is a living example of the penalty of
thought. The brain of this smart little man
has been playing so long and so remorselessly
on his nerves, that they have at last grown
unfit for use. Coffee and tobacco, too,
have done their part, and have converted
this sallow being into a bundle of shuddering
sensibilities. Because I talk of being in love,
because I dare to dream of marrying, he
believes that I wish him to be gone. He
transforms my hopes into hints ; and fearful,
perhaps, of a direct dismissal which would
convulse his dignity with mortification, and
leave his nerves flabby and toneless for ever,
he bids me understand that he considers
his duties at an end. But he'll get over
this pique. Those keen eyes, that pungent

tongue, are the harbingers of no silly spirit.
He will contrast this house with his attic
in Berners Street, this sweet air with the
yellow element of London, his meagre
meals with his present bountiful repasts, and
will discover no urgent necessity to depart.
For myself, I doubt if I could better him.
Use has fathered one or two angularities,
and I find him now not only agreeable, but
necessary."

But, to be candid, these thoughts did
not long trouble me. I had my beautiful
neighbour to muse on, and she was an
inspiration that fully filled my mind.

Three days passed before I saw her
again.

Martelli had gone to Cliffegate for a
walk : I amused myself in the garden. The
grounds were now in complete order. In
the front the fountain had been repaired and
redecorated, and now tossed its pearl-shower
in the sun, circling the cool and brimming

basin with a rainbow. In the back, the trees hung heavy with fruit. The beds were draped with flowers. The lawn, shorn and trimmed to velvet smoothness, offered a pleasant relief to the eye.

I strolled to the end of the grounds and inspected the brilliant *coup d'œil.* My thoughts went further than I: I wished I could have followed them !

"She who loves flowers so well, what would she think of this brilliant show? Were I to ask her to come and see my grounds, would she come?"

At that moment I heard her voice calling to the servant from the garden. An idea struck me. I pushed open the gate and entered the fields. Through the gate of her own garden I could see her. She was raking a bed of geraniums. Her fair face was shadowed by a hat, broad-brimmed and high-crowned ; inelegant it would have looked on many a woman ; but the most fastidious taste would have been ravished by its becoming elegance on her. The skirt of her dress, pinned up, disclosed a foot matchless in its turn and shape. What grace was in the movement of her arms! how delicate the outline of her inclined form! A long curl of gold had slipped from the blue ribbon that bound her hair and reposed like a sunbeam on her back. I stood watching her with all my soul in my gaze. A lark rose shrilling from the fields, and soared, pouring its throat in a strain chastened by the nimble air. She drew herself erect, and protecting her eyes, sought the bird in the blue. Her full and shapely form, her black and luminous eyes, shaded by her hand of snow, her yellow hair, her looped skirt, her firm small feet, made, as she stood among the flowers, such a picture of colour, beauty, and sunshine as I must never hope to see again.

I drew to the gate.

"Good afternoon, Mrs. Fraser," I said gently.

She started, and seeing me, stared without speaking.

"I hope I have not alarmed you," I said, observing the startled expression of her eyes to brighten with a sudden angry light: "I was attracted by the sound of your voice, and would not miss this chance of seeing you."

She let fall the rake and came to the gate.

"How long have you been there?" she asked.

"Some minutes," I replied.

"Watching! watching! Mr. Thorburn, I am sorry you ever took Elmore Court. Before you came, my privacy here was as sacred as though this garden had been cloisters."

"Have I violated it?"

"Of course you have. Have you not been watching me?"

"I must offer you no apology. If I desire to win your approbation, I must not cloud or varnish my meaning."

"It would not be worth while."

"So I will admit that I came here not only with the intention of seeing, but of speaking to you. Now is my crime very grave?"

"Are you beginning to feel dull?" she asked, eyeing me with embarrassing earnestness. "Are your beginning to grow weary of books and thoughts, and to discover that the most tiresome and indiscreet companion a man can choose is himself? If so, why do you not return to London? You must have the means to purchase the distractions which are called pleasures."

"Indeed"—I began.

"Or," she went on with odd imperturbability, "if you can't conveniently leave Elmore Court, there are, I believe, people here whom you might easily get to know. Why me, Mr. Thorburn? why *me?*" she exclaimed, with a little stamp of her foot.

" Who are the people, Mrs. Fraser?"

"Oh, I don't know," she said wearily, " I have never inquired. I have shunned them always. Some of them called. I have their cards by me somewhere. But I never returned their visits."

" And I have some of their cards by me too ; and I have never returned their calls. Such society as they offer does not suit me. Besides, I didn't come here for society."

" But you seek mine."

" I cannot help it," I said.

She left the gate. I thought she was going away. She picked a flower—a white rose, half budded—and brought it me.

" This is of my own planting," said she, applying the pearly petals to her delicate nostrils : " all the flowers that you see here are of my own planting."

" That bud should symbolise your life, Mrs. Fraser."

She opened wide her eyes.

" Why ?" she asked.

" It is unfolding its beauty and sweetness to other eyes than its own. So should you."

She flung it from her. Her under lip pouted as though she were about to cry.

" If I had thought that flower would have provoked so silly a remark, I would not have picked it," she said.

She retired a step. Fearful that I had offended and that she would leave me, I said boldly, " I wish you would allow me to see your flowers. I may learn some hints for my own garden from yours. I faithfully promise not to be poetical again."

"You may come in," she answered, curving her mouth into a childish smile; "Shall I open the gate?"

"Thank you, I can open it."

I entered.

"Please don't notice anything from where you stand," she exclaimed, picking up the rake; "come with me to those steps. My flowers look best from there."

She stepped forward with a light bounding gait. I could observe nothing but her exquisite shape, her yellow hair and alabaster neck. I think, had I held a pair of scissors, that not thrice the number of sylphs and gnomes which protected the perfumed locks of the matchless Belinda could have prevented me from ravishing the amber curl that floated on her back.

She stood on the steps of the door.

"There," cried she, looking up at me with the prettiest smile in the world, "now you will see that all the tints are meant to blend. The roses are not blown yet; but you can guess how pretty they will look next to that bed of lilies. My garden will be a rainbow of colours next month. All the hues meet and melt into one another— from that bed down there to the hedge."

" Beautiful !" I murmured, thinking of her eyes.

" If it were not for my flowers," said she, with a sudden gravity, which did not surprise me, for I was prepared now for any change of mood in this capricious, strange and fascinating woman, " I think I should go mad. You can't tell how I hate the winter. I lie listening to the complaining winds until they become human shapes craving admittance and shelter from the piercing cold. There is a winter's wind that blows here with a strange cry ! . . . Do you think the winds spirits ? I do some-

times, Mr. Thorburn ; nothing else, you
see, sobs and cries like they do. But who
would not scream to be pierced through
and through with hail, wrapped in the
burning lightning, and shattered by the
hateful thunder ?"

She paused, lifting her luminous eyes to
me. "You have read a good deal," said
she, "and will know more than I. Do,
please, tell me what spirits do in winter,
when the air is so frozen it cannot blow,
and when the stars have gone out under the
clouds."

"I assure you," I said, puzzling myself
to reconcile her language with her eyes,
which seemed to me brilliant with intelligence, "I have never studied these matters.
I know nothing of them. They are idle
speculations, and you should not indulge in
them. They will make your solitude very
oppressive."

"They make my solitude more than oppressive at times. But if the winds are tormented spirits, those flowers are good angels. They give me as much pleasure as the winds give me pain. All those flowers have souls. I am quite sure of that. But it is not pleasant to think, for I fear one morning I shall find them all dead through their souls having taken wing."

She pushed some transparent hairs behind her ear.

"I wish, Mrs. Fraser," I said, "you would do me the favour to inspect my garden. I employ two gardeners; but the three of us do not approach you in the delicacy of your taste."

"When do you want me to come?"

"Now, if you will."

"Not now. I must have time to consider. I hardly ever leave my house, and then only for a short walk. And did not I tell you that I visit no one?"

" But you will oblige me in this?"

" I am not sure. You have no claims on me that I should favour you more than any one else. I will think over it, and tell you to-morrow. Will you come to watch me again at the gate?"

" If I may?"

" Oh, you *may*. The fields are not mine; and I have no right to forbid trespassers."

" I will come to the gate at the hour I met you to-day."

" Yes."

" And you will accompany me over my grounds."

" I shall see. Now I must go in."

She held out her hand, I took and retained it.

" Before I leave you, Mrs. Fraser, will

you tell me that my society is not distasteful
—that you no longer look upon me as an
intruder ?"

She did not offer to withdraw her hand.
It seemed to me, indeed, that she hardly
knew I held it.

"No. I am disposed to like you," she
replied. "You weren't frank at first ; but
you have become frank since, and that
makes you a pleasant companion. Oh!
you will never know my abhorrence of the
cant which politeness makes men and women
talk. They treat each other like cats—
stroke, and stroke, until truth is lost in a
general purring. I like truthful people.
They need not be insulting : they can
always keep back unpleasant knowledge;
but they need not *lie*. Polite people *must*
lie."

I would not argue. It pleased me better
to watch the varying expressions of her

beautiful face, the soft curvings of her lips, the graceful gestures of her hands, than to contradict.

"Good-bye," she said.

"Until to-morrow," I answered.

Near the gate I halted to pick up the rose-bud she had thrown from her, and pressed it to my lips. Peeping furtively toward the house, I saw she watched me from the window.

CHAPTER IV.

I SAID next day to Martelli, " You will see Mrs. Fraser this afternoon, I hope. She has half promised to come and look at my flowers."

" What have I to do with Mrs. Fraser?" he exclaimed with a shrug. " My business is with books, not women. I can understand the one, but not the other."

" But I want to justify my love. Her beauty will do this for me."

" Have I not seen her?" he asked, stretching out his arms.

" Yes, by moonlight—with blank eyes

and expressionless face.   Her beauty by noon
is somewhat different from her beauty by
night."

" Sir, yellow hair and black eyes make no
charm for me."

" You are a Goth."

" When I was a young man I fell in love
once a week.   That proves a catholic taste,
at all events, for my Hebes must have
varied."

" But you will let me introduce you to
Mrs. Fraser? You can know and like
without admiring her.   You will be struck
with her conversation."

" Does she talk well ?"

" She talks strangely—what Shakespeare
calls ' matter and impertinency mixed.'
Her shrewd discursiveness pleases me."

" Ah, Sir, you are willing to be
pleased."

" I cannot help being pleased.   Her

musical prattle is very different from the sort of entertainment I am used to in other women. Dull decorous reason I can get anywhere. *Her* talk is rare as her beauty."

" A kind of mad talk, Sir."

" Mad, indeed! You shall hear her yourself and judge."

" Pray excuse me. I will take my pipe, and while you enjoy your *tête-à-tête* will search for curious objects on the beach."

" Be it so, then," said I, somewhat chagrined: for I wanted to witness this chilly sceptic melting into admiration before my beautiful neighbour's eyes.

There goes a disappointed man (thought I, as I watched him enter the house). His austerity cloaks some odd experience, I dare swear. Could I but see into his memory I might witness a strange drama being played in that little theatre. Some

unconscionable jilt has soured the ripe juices
of his nature; and now he spits venom at
the whole sex. Yet he makes wry faces
over his cynicism. I don't think he relishes
it much. He argues, I suppose, that the
coming of a wife will prove the going of
his occupation. He has a rich young fellow
under his charge and has no wish to surrender him to the keeping of a woman.
So he directs his forked tongue at her in
the hope that I shall be influenced. My
little signor, you will be disappointed, if
you hope this!

He left the house after lunch.

At the proper hour I stood at the gate
in the fields and peeped over. The garden
was empty. I looked at my watch. It was
past the time at which I had met her the
day before. Twenty minutes passed. I
walked to and fro, staring at the windows
in the hope of catching a glimpse of her

face. Believing she would disappoint me, I grew irritable. " Her conduct," I thought, " is unladylike, to say the least. She promised to meet me, and should come. If she is making a fool of me how will that Martelli exult! But it is my own fault. Am I not an independent man? If I want to marry, have I not but to open my arms to have them filled without the trouble of wooing? For how many women are there who would not cheerfully do all the courting for two thousand pounds a year? Then what do I here, in a hot field, tormented by that accursed gnat" (and here I aimed a prodigious but idle blow at the insect) " worrying my mind with conjectures, a spectacle for the pert eye of the widow's maid, who probably sits watching me from the ambush of a window-curtain?" And I was positively in the act of walking away, when suddenly, from amid a row of lilac

trees close to the gate, stepped forth—Mrs.
Fraser.

"Shall I tell you your thoughts?" she
exclaimed, approaching me, without re-
turning my salutation by smile or bow.

"If you please," I answered, my mood
clearing in her presence as the cloudy
heavens clear when the sun shines out.

"Stoop your ear then."

I inclined my head. She leaned across
the gate and whispered, "Mrs. Fraser——
Oh!" she cried, springing back, and clapping her hands, "there are some words that
are coarse and burning in the mouth as
radishes. This is one. But it's true—and
truth must be pungent."

"But before I can tell whether it is
true or not, let me know what you
think."

"Don't you think me—a humbug?"

"No, no!" I exclaimed with a laugh.

"Why do you say no?" with sudden earnestness.

"But I may tell you I was annoyed," I continued, "because I feared you would not come."

"I expected you would be, and so I determined to watch you. *You* watched me yesterday. It was not fair. When one is alone one indulges in all kinds of moods; and you might have seen me make myself ugly and foolish by pouting, grimacing, frowning, or smiling, just as the mood obliged me. I don't like to be caught unawares. I choose to smooth my face down so," looking gravely, "when I am watched. There is an expression I wear as a vizor; it's this."

As a three-year old child looks, who, being told not to smile, frowns, that it may appear grave, so looked she. Then, breaking into a sudden smile:

"I watched you frown. You stared at my poor little house as though you could have burnt it up with your eyes. How you flung your impatience at the tiny fly that annoyed you! 'Oh this treacherous woman!' you thought; 'how glibly she made the word of promise to the ear to break it to the hope!' Did you not think all this and as much more as would take me twenty minutes to tell? I watched you just as steadily as you watched me yesterday. I saw your weakness. Did you see mine? No—my hat hid my face. You couldn't see my eyes. And unless you see the eyes you can't tell what is going on in the mind."

"No, nor when you see the eyes can you always tell what is going on. It would be a delightful privilege," said I, looking steadily at her, "to be able to interpret those fiery hieroglyphics in which the soul writes her thoughts upon the eyes."

"I don't think so," she replied. "There would be little pleasure in life if we could read one another's thoughts."

"There would be no hypocrisy, at all events; we should have to speak the truth."

"And would you like that?" she asked. "Would the plain heiress like to hear her lover declare that his only motive in offering her marriage was to get her money? Would the father like to hear that the reason of his son's affection is that he may not be forgotten in his will. Life is a great mirage. Let it alone—pray, let it alone. Don't pour the light of truth on it, or it will vanish like a rainbow when the storm is over."

"I thought, Mrs. Fraser, you were so enamoured of truth?"

"Yes, among my friends. It pleases me to speak the truth, and I choose to hear the truth spoken. I hate compliments, and fine language, and the gingerbread splendour of *politeness*, as it is called. But it is not because I love truth that I would rob the world, which I hate, of the pleasure of telling lies."

"You spoke of my weakness just now. What weakness did my face or behaviour illustrate?"

"Impatience."

"Nothing worse?"

"If I had remarked anything worse, I should have let you go away."

"Allow me to open this gate. You will come and see my flowers?"

"It would not be fair in me to refuse you after keeping you waiting so long."

I held the gate open. She passed from her garden into mine.

"These grounds present no such pretty

coup d'œil as yours," I said. "I am new at this sort of work, and for all I know my taste may be a little cockneyfied."

"Oh, but the garden is in beautiful order! Pray do not speak to me of my poor little slip of ground. That lawn is larger." We paced through the walks. I could hardly remove my eyes from her face. She had replaced her hat of yesterday by one resembling that worn by Peg Woffington in Reynolds's picture. Her dress was black silk, with a muslin body. A carved ivory cross hung on her bosom by a chain of white coral.

"Your presence here gives me great happiness," I exclaimed; " and it makes me proud to think that I should have been the first to cause you to break through your rule of solitude."

"I have lived here a long time now, and you are the only person I know," she answered.

"But you must have felt dull some-times?"

"Often.   How should I help feeling dull? I have no one to speak to."

"But this must be your own fault," I said gently.   "You might easily have made acquaintances."

"Yes, but I would not risk it.   I might not like them, and in a small place like this it is embarrassing to withdraw from society after one has mingled in it.   Besides, people are apt to be impertinent when they have nothing to do.   A widow is always an object of curiosity, especially to elderly spinsters— and there are many here.   Now I will let any one discuss me to her heart's content— on one condition : that we remain strangers. Oh, what a glorious rose, Mr. Thor-burn!"

I separated it from the tree and gave it to her.

"You should have offered it more timidly," she exclaimed, looking at me over the flower; "how did you know I would not reject it like I did your bouquet?"

"I didn't think. But you recall my wish to send you some flowers. Will you let me order the gardener to make you a bouquet?"

"If you please."

I called to one of the men and gave him the instructions. We got upon the lawn.

"What a pretty house!" she said, looking up. "It stands so cool and white from the road. What made you take it?"

"I got tired of London. I wanted to study."

"Oh, I remember—you told me. Do you study now?"

"Not much, I fear."

"Where do you study?"

"In my library there," said I, pointing to the window.

"You ought to be there now. I am keeping you from your books," she exclaimed, with a certain grave archness.

"You would be keeping me from my books, whether you were absent or present."

"Should I? How?"

"By making me think of you."

"And do you really think of me, Mr. Thorburn?"

"You have never been out of my mind since the evening I dreamt of you."

"It was curious you should have dreamed of me," she said, putting her hands behind her and leaning against the back of a garden-seat.

"It was mysterious," I answered gravely.

"And was my face in your dream exactly like it is here?" she asked, looking up that I might see her fully.

"It was more sad. You had a broken-hearted look in your eyes. What I saw in my dream was more like your face in your sleep, when I met you afterwards."

"What made you dream of me?"

"I cannot tell."

"Had you ever seen me?"

"Never."

"Nor heard me described?"

"No."

"How quickly the swallows fly!" she exclaimed, pointing in the air. "What would you give to be able to live all day long in that pure blue? This is a beautiful rose you have given me. How can the thick, ugly, common earth yield such lovely things?"

"You were questioning me, Mrs. Fraser. Do continue your examination."

"Questioning you? What about?" she asked, looking at me with a little bewildered air.

" About my dream. I have often wanted to discuss it with you, that I may understand it. You who inspired it should know what it means."

" I cannot tell you, indeed. I did not inspire it. I had never seen you nor heard of you."

" In the olden times it was the custom to examine dreams, in the belief that they were prophecies. I would like to revive the custom, to see what my dream forebodes."

" What should it forebode? Sadness, perhaps, since my eyes were so sad."

" Dreams go by contraries, they say."

" Then they are useless as prophecies."

" But I am by no means disposed to let my dream slip by so easily. I choose to think it significant in some sense which I wish explained."

"It was a prophecy, perhaps, that you should meet me : and you did."

"It was a prophecy perhaps, that our lives were to mingle, and they may."

"Nothing is impossible," she answered quietly.

She did not say this consciously. It was an answer obviously made without the slightest reference to its implication.

"How beautiful these grounds of yours look under the blue sky," she continued gaily. "I wish you had not made me see them. They will spoil me for my narrow garden."

"Why will you not use them as your own? Those gates were made for communication. You can always be alone by naming the hours it may suit you to come. I can dismiss the gardeners for that time, and hide myself in my study."

"Your offer is very polite, but I will not

accept it. I shouldn't care to wander about
a place that doesn't belong to me; for there
is little real satisfaction in admiring the
possessions of others. Besides, my fingers
would itch to be at the flowers. I should
be picking the choicest. That is my
way."

"You would be welcome to pick them
all."

"Yet were I to come I would not wish
you to hide yourself. Your company does
me good. I have felt more cheerful since I
knew you."

"You give me great pleasure in saying
this, Mrs. Fraser."

"I mean it. I find you frank and easy
and kind. You are not in the least tiresome. When you first spoke to me I saw
your face set out with compliments and
mots, like any other man's might have been.
But I swept this sugary French repast away

and made you substitute hearty nourishing solids. This makes you agreeable."

Her grave innocent look forbade me to smile; yet it was not easy to preserve my gravity. I felt like a big boy lectured by some pretty little girl.

She stood looking pensively at her foot, which she waved to and fro on the heel; then exclaimed,

" I am going now."

I had no wish to part with her.

" Pray don't go yet. We have not been long together."

" No, not very long. But taste is refined by abstinence."

" Yes, but this sort of refinement is fretting. Your company is like that sweet wine, mentioned by a Persian poet, of which the more you drank the thirstier you became."

" Oh ! here comes the gardener with my bouquet !" she cried.

The man presented it to her, cap in hand.

"Thank you, thank you," she exclaimed, inclining her sweet face over the flowers. And when the man had withdrawn, she drew close to me, and pointing with a white finger to the bouquet, said :

"Have you ever imagined what shapes and expressions the spirits of flowers take? The spirit of the lily would be a languid floating shape, with meek eyes and hands crossed on her bosom : but of course very, very small—smaller than the fairies. The violet would be a little baby boy with round blue eyes and a wee red mouth. The rose would be a young girl with a rich complexion. Her beautiful limbs would be tinted with a delicate pink like the shadow of the red rose in water. She would be haughty, with a glowing eye; and her hair would be bound by a circle of gold."

"And what flower," I asked, "should, at its death, take the form of a woman exquisitely modelled, with black eyes melting from one sweet expression into another, sometimes startled, sometimes pleading, always luminous with bright but tender alternations of thought"——

"I see," she interrupted gravely; "you agree with me; you believe in the resurrection of the flowers."

"I think you could make me believe in anything."

She uttered a laugh; its abruptness made it discordant.

"Good-bye," she exclaimed, "I will come and see your flowers again some day."

"May I not show you over my house?"

"What is there to be seen?"

"Come and judge."

I held the door open; she paused, entered, and returned.

"I'll not look over your house to-day. You have had enough of my company. You may walk with me to the gate."

She moved away, I followed her.

"How long do you think my bouquet will last, Mr. Thorburn?"

"Some days."

"I wonder that people who like one another should make presents of flowers. When a young man presents a bouquet to the girl he is in love with, do either of them think that the gift exactly typifies their passion—all human passion—which is bright to-day and withered to-morrow?"

"They would hardly think this. I can understand love seeking for expression in the most lovely and fragrant symbols the world has to offer. But the real truth is, the majority of lovers don't think at all.

They imitate. They give what others give."

"Now that is the way I like to hear people talk," she exclaimed with a merry laugh ; "I am quite sure that the only way to be truthful is to be cynical."

"I am afraid so."

"If I were a young and inexperienced girl, the person on whose judgment I should most depend would be the one who most sincerely disbelieved in the existence of virtue."

"No, no. Such an infidel would make a bad guide."

"An infallible guide, you mean. How could he err ?"

"He would err by not being able to grasp the full character of the world's wickedness. He would underrate its depravity by allowing it no virtue whatever."

"I don't understand. This is a paradox," said she stopping, for we had reached the gate. "Would you increase the world's wickedness by making it virtuous?"

"Yes, up to a certain point. I speak in the sense of Dean Swift, who said we had all of us Christianity enough to make us hate one another. Virtue has a very fructifying power, and vice springs richly from its soil. A totally wicked world is an impossibility. That dreadful place to which we are told sinners will be consigned cannot be utterly wicked, or it could not exist."

"I almost catch your meaning, but you don't express yourself well, Mr. Thorburn."

"You are quite right. I am given, I am sorry to say, to walking round my thoughts too much." I could have added that such eyes as hers were not calculated to make a man logical or even disputatious, save in a love argument.

"I am then to believe that there is enough good in the world to make it more wicked than it would be were there no good?"

"Why, having advanced my position, I am bound to stick to it. You have said indeed what I think, but what I would not preach."

She stood lost in thought for some moments.

"Mr. Thorburn," she presently said, "I think the world very, very bad ; it is cold-hearted, selfish, and dishonourable and mean and pitiless. I see now that it could not be all this if it had not what it calls virtue and religion to prompt it ; for the virtue of the world teaches us to hate those whom it pronounces corrupt ; and its religion"——— she stopped with a bewildered look ; "what does its religion teach?"

"History will answer that better than

I. But what have we to do with the world, Mrs. Fraser? Here, under that tender sky, amid these flowers, fanned by this soft air, we should not let thoughts of its wrongs and treacheries trouble us."

"If one could throw memory upon the air and bid the breeze bear its burden a thousand miles away, then would it be well. But the afternoon is passing. Good-bye, Mr. Thorburn."

"When may I see you again?"

"Oh, you will find a time," she answered with a little demure laugh; and so saying she passed through the gate.

CHAPTER V.

HER manners, her moods, her beauty had fascinated me. My love for her was become a passion. I determined before long to declare it. But before doing so, I resolved to see more of her. I wanted to be sure that she loved me before I proposed. I felt my happiness would be staked on the issue of the offer, and dreaded the result of hasty action.

You may believe I thought very hard over the problem of her nature; but I could arrive at no solution that satisfied me. She had affirmed that she liked my company; but the assurance had been too much qualified by the *naïveté* of the declaration to be pleasing. A better illustration, at least a more satisfactory indication, lay in her not avoiding me.

But what an odd character was hers! How inadequate is language to represent her! I can only give you the bare uncoloured outline. It is beyond my power to fill it up with the details which must be accurately painted, before you can have before you, as I knew her, my beautiful, wayward, fantastical, child-like neighbour.

I suppose my love blinded me, or I should have attached more importance to the various little perplexing points of character which stole out during our conversations. Her candour was made too piquant by her eyes, her downright utterances too musical by her voice, her rapid divergence from one topic to another too pretty by the infantine air that accompanied it, to suffer me to note any other meaning than that which met the eye and ear.

I laid aside my books and my ambitions in my pursuit of her. Compared with winning her, all other pleasures and hopes were poor and small indeed. My love engrossed my thoughts, held me absent; and made me altogether more foolish than my sense of self-respect will suffer me to recall.

She was right when she told me I should find a time to meet her. I met her the next day. I met her the day after; and upon succeeding days again. Once I prevailed upon her to accompany me in a walk to the cliffs, by an unfrequented road leading to a spot where we stood in little danger of being intruded on. It was on this occasion that I witnessed in her more constrained air, in her speech more suave than usual, in her eyes which were sometimes

shyly averted, the presence of an emotion
I had waited for and sought to excite.
The breakers creamed at our feet; a west
wind cooled the air; the white gulls swept
by on curved and steady wings; the sun
reared an unbroken silver pillar in the
sea. The scene, the sounds, the solitude
were propitious to love; but I would not
speak my feelings yet. I felt that the
memory of this calm and tender hour we
were passing together would do more
for me than I could do for myself.

During the week Martelli and I had been
little together. My mind had been too
much employed with hopes and fears of
its own to suffer me to remark him
attentively; but I had noticed that he had
been to the full as abstracted as I. But his
abstraction was of a gloomy order. His
dark eyes, his contracted brow, his set
lips, proclaimed the sullenness of his
thoughts.

I attributed his manner to my neglect
of him, and to his resentment at being
invited to a position which had been de-
spoiled of its duties. I must confess my
love may have impaired my politeness. I
was no longer the attentive host, solicitous
of his comfort, and on the *qui vive* to
remove any unpleasant thoughts which his
position would inspire, and which his language, indeed, would sometimes hint. But
I could easily excuse my neglect, if neglect
it were. It was not to be supposed that
I could regard him altogether in the light
of a guest. Or granting that I chose to do
so, his long stay in my house would have
justified a mitigation of the severe politeness
which it would have been proper to extend
to a man whose sojourn was brief.
"Surely," I remember thinking, "under
the circumstances, he should have sense
enough at this time of day not to expect

from me the anxious attention which I readily practised at the beginning of our acquaintance. I have fulfilled conditions which he could not have anticipated. I have suffered him to share my home as though he were a joint proprietor; and I have tacitly conceded every privilege which I could with justice to myself yield to him. I cannot consider him ill-used because I choose to absent myself in the company of Mrs. Fraser, in preference to spending my time with him. He no doubt frets and fumes at my love as indiscreet—as menacing his situation, and as illustrative of weakness in a nature that had at the onset promised a vigorous adherence to its original schemes. But surely," I thought, "it will be time enough for him to manifest anger when he shall have been told that I have abandoned my ambitious resolutions and no longer require his counsels."

On reaching home after that walk I have told you of with Mrs. Fraser, I found Martelli seated on the lawn. I joined him. He rose at my approach. His politeness was punctilious in proportion to his temper.

" Pray keep your seat," said I. " How have you been passing the afternoon?"

" In reading," he answered with a shrug.

" You say that reproachfully. You think I should be reading too?"

" Are you not master of your own actions, Sir?"

" Undoubtedly. I shall resume my reading by-and by."

"I hope so, for your own sake. You are abandoning a fine future."

" Why do you say that? My future is still mine. I have not abandoned it. I have still my schemes and my hopes. I shall try to realise them."

" You will never realise them, Sir, if you

allow your mind to be diverted by the first small attraction that happens to rise."

"Small attraction! But I can forgive you. You are a scholar, a student, a recluse—what should you know of love?"

His eyes shone.

"Nothing! nothing! I am ignorant of the passion," he exclaimed, flourishing his hand.

"Yet I should have taken you to be too wise a man to have neglected cultivating your sympathies in the direction where the most provocation lies. Love is so human a passion, its consequences are so manifold, its influences so remarkable, that were you anything of a philosopher you would have made it a study. How can you hope to understand men, when you are ignorant of the great master-passion of humanity?"

"How do you know I am so ignorant as you think me?"

"I judge so by the sneers you are disposed to level at love, and by the light contemptuous manner with which you treat it."

"May not that prove that I know too much?"

"I don't see how. Cynicism is of superficial growth. Deep knowledge makes one grave and compassionate. The painter knew life who gave a smirk to the fool and sadness to the sage."

"But it is to be expected of a man who has sounded this passion to its bottom that he should ridicule the belief in its depth, when he knows it to be shallow."

"Give me leave to push your metaphor. If you speak of yourself, you probably got among the shoals, and inferred from your soundings that the deep was everywhere shallow."

He gave one of his shrugs and sat silent. I took out my cigar-case and held it open to him. He declined with a wave of his hand. I glanced at his face; it was hard and angry.

" Martelli," said I, " you are too sensitive. What has vexed you?"

" How am I sensitive, Sir?" he asked, growing a shade pale.

" I cannot tell you *how* you are sensitive," I replied, stirred a little by the suppressed irritation of his voice; " but I think I can guess the cause of your vexation."

" Pray tell me, Sir."

" You think I am neglecting you for Mrs. Fraser?"

He gave a fierce nod.

" And you are disposed to resent my placing you in so anomalous a position as that which you now occupy?"

" Sir, never mind that. I admit you have disappointed me."

" I am sorry I cannot see how."

"How should you see? You are blinded by love."

"Signor Martelli, I must beg you to calm yourself. I cannot suffer such language as this."

"But, Sir, you provoke me!" he exclaimed, gesticulating and growing yet paler. "You raise expectations to disappoint them. When I came here, I secretly pledged myself to carry you through any schemes you had a mind to indulge. All my diligence, my time, my knowledge, my patience, I meant to give to you. I liked you, Sir. Your manners pleased me. It was charming to attend one so acute and so humble—so quick to perceive and so eager to be taught. And I too had my ambitions! They are gone."

"They are not gone, Martelli," I said, softened.

"They are, Sir!" he cried, clenching

both fists. "It is a blow. I am a poor
man. Had you let me do for you what I
could have done, you would have requited
me. Of that I am sure. Yes, Sir; I am
not so ignorant of human nature as not to
tell generosity when I see it; and yours is a
generous mind. It made me this promise:
it said, 'Martelli, serve me well, advance
my schemes, impart the knowledge and the
power your experience and learning can inspire, and when I have achieved the ends I
covet I will reward you.' That is what you
told me, Sir."

"But what did you expect?"

"As much as it was in your power to
confer. You would not have forgotten the
man who gave you help when you needed it.
You might have made me your secretary—
your agent—your amanuensis. You would
have invented some post for me to fill—you
would, at least, have rescued me from a life

of drudgery. But now, I am forced back again upon my pitiful calling—teaching at schools, soliciting pupils, and starving as a teacher !"

" I see no necessity. Have I dismissed you ?"

" I dismiss myself !" he cried, standing up and striking his chest with his fist.

I was impressed by his vehemence ; at once pained and made curious by his manner.

" At all events," I said, " if you go, you go of your own accord."

" Of course," he replied sarcastically.

" But at the same time you will allow me to say that I think you foolish for exhibiting so much impatience."

" Impatience !" he exclaimed, with a sharp laugh. " Oh, no! I am not impatient. But, Sir, it is not pleasant to be given to drink of a wine that is dashed from your lips after you have tasted enough to like its sweetness." .

"But, my dear fellow, nobody *has* dashed the wine away, that I can see."

"You have! you have!" he cried, with a grin of anger.

"I? You are dreaming."

"*Sacramento!* don't tell me I dream!"

"I shall have to tell you something worse," said I, getting up; "if you don't moderate your temper, I shall have to tell you that you are mad."

"That it should come to this!" he muttered, looking up, as though he apostrophised the air.

"You speak English fluently," said I; "let me entreat you to express yourself intelligibly that I may understand your grievance."

He left me; walked to the edge of the

lawn, returned, approached close to me, and said,

" It is your intention, Sir, to marry, is it not ?"

" What of that ?"

" When, Sir, do you marry ?"

" I shall probably make the lady an offer to-morrow," I answered, compressing my lips to disguise a smile.

" Ah !" He nodded fiercely, walked once more to the edge of the lawn, and returned. " You are serious, Sir? You really mean to marry ?"

I could not help laughing out, as I answered, " Yes."

" Then, Sir, pay me what you owe me, and let me go."

" Do you wish to leave at once?"

" At once !" he cried.

" Very well; come with me to the library.

I will reckon what I am in your debt and pay you."

He followed me into the house. I seated myself at the writing-table. But hardly believing it possible he could be in earnest, or wishing at least to make one more effort to conciliate him, I said,

" Will you not defer this matter until to-morrow ?   Take to-night to think over your resolution.   This kind of separation is very ungracious and unpleasant.   I really do not wish you to go.   I have told you before I like your company, and have found you most valuable.   I repeat it now."

" But you are going to marry ?"

" What of that ?   After my marriage we will continue our reading."

" But you are going to marry ?" he repeated.

" Good heaven !   Do you think Mrs. Fraser an ogress ?   Do you think she will eat you? When you know her you will like her." He shook his head furiously, and violently waved his hand before his face.

" Pay me, Sir, pay me, and let me go!" he exclaimed.

Disgusted by his irritable perversity, I drew out my cheque-book.

" Can you not pay me in gold?" he asked.

" Certainly, if you prefer it. But first let me see what I owe you."

I took a slip of paper and made my calculations; then went to an iron safe, drew out a cash-box and gave him the money.

" There," said I, " is the discharge of your proper claims. But I owe you some-- thing for the interest you have taken in me and the hearty industry you have employed on my behalf. This will perhaps make my gratitude more significant than were I to express it in words only."

And I handed a bank note for twenty pounds.

He took, folded, and put it in his pocket.

"I am obliged to you, Sir," he said, with a low bow, "but in taking it, it is 'my poverty, but not my will, consents.'"

"Shall my servant carry your portmanteau?"

"Thank you, no; it is not heavy. I can carry it myself."

"The phaeton is at your service, if you wish to drive to Cornpool."

"I will walk, Sir."

I held out my hand, but pretending not to notice the action he gave me another low bow and left the room. In less than twenty minutes I saw him walk, portmanteau in hand, down the front garden.

Thus ended my connection with this singular little man.

CHAPTER VI.

Had I had nothing else to do but to read and muse I should have greatly missed Martelli. As it was, I felt his absence on the evening that followed his departure. I missed his dark face, his glowing eye, his rapid speech, his tart questions. His arm-chair looked very empty without him. My supper too was somewhat tasteless, wanting the sharp condiment of his tongue and gestures. But how should I feel his absence very sensibly with Mrs. Fraser to comfort me? I only wonder I felt it at all. Our parting had not been calculated to sharpen regret. I had no notion he was such a passionate man. There was no doubt he had been insulting. But what in the world could have provoked such an outbreak? He would have had me believe it was my resolution to marry Mrs. Fraser that angered him. But what was Mrs. Fraser to him? Was he a monomaniac—mad on the subject of women? We know that there are people born with antipathies which nothing can shake. Lady Heneage would faint at the sight of a rose; the Marquis de la Roche-jacquelin would turn white with fear before a squirrel; and I have read in some author of a man whose antipathy to old women was such, that once when his friends, by way of joke, introduced an elderly female into his presence, he fell in a fit and died. I do not say that I quite believed this to be Martelli's disease: but I was strongly disposed to think that he had some eccentric aversion to living in a house where there was a mistress.

I did not pass a quiet night. I had resolved to propose next day to my beautiful neighbour, and my resolution rather agitated me. A man may do in a moment of impulse what he would fear to attempt in cold blood. I was rather sorry I had not proposed that afternoon. I had been surrounded by conditions highly favourable to a declaration. It would have been over now, and I should have been able to sleep the sleep of the accepted.

I had told her I would call in the morning. At another time she might have asked me in her odd sweet way "Why?" but her silence was auspicious. She had lowered her beautiful eyes, and the conscious curve of her mouth gave me reason to believe she had guessed my mission.

So at about eleven o'clock, when the sun

stood high and the land lay hot and still beneath its fiery gaze, I took my hat and stepped over to Elmore Cottage. There was no need of ceremony now to gain admittance. The girl knew I was a privileged visitor and admitted me with a smile.

I entered the little drawing-room. It was empty. The blinds were half drawn, and the window stood wide open. Signs of her recent presence were visible in the garden hat upon the sofa, in some drawing materials on the table, above all, in the soft peculiar perfume which I associated with her. She was such a strange woman that I thought she might have hidden on hearing my knock ; and I looked behind the sofa, and the door, and in the corner protected by the piano, for her. Then I drew to the table to see what she was drawing. It was a man's head, unfinished though complete enough to offer a good likeness. The hair was dark, the nose straight, the mouth firm, the eye sufficiently large. The slight line of whisker was not shaded. This sketch dissipated all my nervousness. I looked up with a smile, and met her eyes peering at me from the door.

"If I had known it was you I should have hid that," said she, coming forward in a somewhat defiant manner, but with a delicate pink on her cheek.

"Did you not want me to see it?"

"No."

"Why? It is charmingly done—the very image of me."

She came round to where I stood.

"Go and stand opposite," she said, "and then I shall be able to tell."

I did as she bade me.

"Hold your face in profile."

I looked at the wall. She was silent for some moments.

" Yes. It is not bad. My memory must be good."

" Mrs. Fraser," said I, " what made you take my face for a subject ?"

" Are you annoyed ?"

" No; and you don't think me annoyed ?"

" Oh, I fancied you would think I had not flattered you enough."

" But what made you take my face ?"

" Because it suited me."

I placed a chair for her and seated myself at her side.

" Mrs. Fraser, I know your Christian name—it is Geraldine. May I call you Geraldine ?"

" How did you know that ?" she asked suddenly.

" I read it at the corner of those drawings there."

She laughed.

" May I call you Geraldine ?"

"If you like. Do you think it a pretty name?"

"A sweet name. Now, Geraldine, will you tell me what made you take my face for a sketch?"

The utterance of her name pleased her. She looked up at me with lighted eyes.

"Have I not told you?"

"No. Your answer was evasive. I want the truth."

"I wished to see if I could hit off its expression with my pencil."

"And you have drawn a good likeness. But I miss one thing."

"What is that?" she asked, getting up and looking at the drawing.

"Look at those eyes," I answered, bending over her and pointing.

"Well; they are bold—do you mean they are not large enough?"

"Oh, they are large enough. But they do not tell the truth."

" What should they tell?"

" My love, Geraldine."

She did not answer. I passed my arm round her waist.

" Do you see what I mean?"

She raised her eyes to my face. I searched them ; they were calm, and pensive and soft, but radiant too, with a light that was new to them.

" I understand," she whispered.

I led her to a chair and knelt by her that I might see her face, holding her hand in both mine.

" Geraldine, you knew that I loved you ?"

" No, I did not know it."

" But you suspected it."

" Yes, I could not help suspecting it."

" And do you love me, Geraldine ?"

" Yes."

" Well enough to be my wife ?"

" Yes."

I kissed her forehead. "How am I to thank you for your love?"

"By always, always, loving me."

"I will always love you, Geraldine."

"I am sure you will," she answered fondly, smoothing my cheek; "and your name is Arthur. May I call you Arthur?"

"Of course you may."

"Arthur," she said, looking earnestly into my eyes, "what makes you want me to be your wife?"

"My love."

"And what makes you love me?"

"Your sweetness—your waywardness— and all the little points and lights, the colour and shadow, which make up your character and your beauty."

"But would you like my character if I were not pretty?"

"Certainly I should."

"You would think me rude. My face is

like charity to my character—it hides my multitude of sins."

"Your face is like music to poetry—it turns your character to song."

"Arthur, you may compliment me now if you like; I shall love to hear your praise."

"Dearest," I exclaimed, rising, "how proud and happy your love makes me feel! Finding you here in this solitude and taking you from it, makes me resemble one of those knights of old who rescued beautiful damsels from the guardianship of the horrible dragons which then flourished. Your dragon is more matter-of-fact than the scaly brutes the poets sing of ; but let me tell you it is quite as formidable. *Ennui* is its name."

"Come into the garden," she exclaimed, springing up ; "I prefer talking in the sunshine."

"Come into my garden," I answered; "there are trees there and we shall like the cool shade." And she tied on her hat before the looking-glass, regarding me with her black eyes, though she seemed to regard herself. I said, "Would you like to live at Elmore Court when we are married?"

"Oh, yes!" she answered, turning quickly round, "I would not choose to live anywhere else."

"But will you not find it dull?"

"Not with you," she replied.

I kissed her hand. "At all events," I said, "we can live there until the term I have taken it for is expired."

"We will live there always," she exclaimed earnestly. "But come into the garden. You can tell how much I care for the world by living here," she continued, as we left the house; "indeed I never wish to see the world again. I will make you promise always to live at Elmore Court, for there we shall be alone. I shall want you all to myself, Arthur. Indeed you will find me jealous, dear—would you like me to be jealous?"

"It is the most genuine test of love. You will find me jealous too."

"Shall I?" she cried, clapping her hands. "And it will be very proper that you should. But I doubt if you'll have occasion."

We passed through the gate and entered the grounds of Elmore Court.

"How could you think I should be dull here?" she asked, prettily folding her hands, whilst she paused to look at the building and the brilliant *coup d'œil* of the garden. "All day long I should be busy with my flowers, and in the evening you should read to me, and teach me all you know, that I may become as wise as you."

" I will show you over the house presently, Geraldine. Meanwhile let us seat ourselves under those trees. Dearest," I said, taking her hand, " I have been so long looking forward to this time, when I may call you and think of you as my own, that now it is come I cannot believe it here."

" You have not had to wait very long. Did you expect to win me so easily ?"

" I don't know; but I felt you would become my wife."

" But I was not destined for you, or I should have married you first. Is it here we are to sit ?"

" We are in the shade here."

She passed her hand through my arm and pressed her shoulder against mine.

" Do you feel happy, Arthur ?"

" Perfectly happy."

" Do you wish to ask me any questions about my past, dearest ?"

"No. If there is anything I should know you will tell me."

She sighed and pressed her cheek against my shoulder.

"Arthur," she .whispered, "my marriage was not a happy one."

"I should have thought that, Geraldine, by your eyes."

"Are they so very mournful?"

"Sometimes. But mournful does not so well define their expression as pensive. Your heart is sometimes troubled."

"With the past," she rejoined quickly and eagerly. "My husband did not love me. He left me. When I became a widow I resolved to bury my sorrow and my life in some quiet obscure corner like Cliffegate. I have a little income, Arthur—why do you not ask me about it? Other men would."

"I hope you will not find me altogether

like other men; though I hope I am no
Pharisee."

"I have two hundred a year. It was left
me by grandmamma. Her solicitor sends
me fifty pounds every quarter. You may
have it all, Arthur."

"Thanks, dear; and in return you shall
have two thousand a year to spend with
me."

"Is that your fortune?" she asked, opening her eyes.

I nodded, with a smile.

"How rich you are! But it is nice to
have plenty of money, and I shan't love
you the less for having it. No; many
women would pretend that they would
much rather have found you poor, that they
might feel sure you knew you were loved
only for yourself. Now I am glad you are
rich; not because I care for your money,
but because I know that such a fortune as

yours must have enabled you to see life, and that your choice of me comes after an experience of the world. It will be a matured choice, so that I shall not be likely to lose you."

" Geraldine, you talk the language of wisdom, as the Turks say. I *have* seen life, and can promise you that my love is not the caprice of a greenhorn."

" Now you shall show me over your house," she said, jumping up.

I conducted her in by the balcony, and when we were in the library I said, " This is the room in which I first saw you."

" Here ?"

" Yes ; I fell asleep, and in that sleep I saw your face."

" Were you frightened, Arthur ?"

" It was only a dream. But I was frightened when I saw you afterwards."

" What a quantity of books you have !"

she exclaimed, standing on tiptoe to read
the backs of the volumes on the upper
shelves. " Have you read them all ?"

" I wish I had. I should be a wiser
man."

" Too wise to marry me, perhaps?"

"The wisdom that would prohibit that
would be very closely allied to insanity. I
have had little reason during my life to flatter
myself on my judgment ; but I think I may
boast of my wisdom now."

" This room is very pretty, and those
grounds look lovely from the window; yet
you must have felt dull here."

" I confess I did—in spite of the entertainment provided for me by a sharp sinister
little foreigner named Martelli, whom I
hired to keep me company—a little man—
humorous, passionate, and I daresay vengeful."

" I dislike foreigners," she said, with a

shudder. "Why did you not employ an Englishman?"

"The fact was, I wished to learn Italian."

"Was he an Italian?" she asked quickly.

"Yes. Don't you like Italians?"

"I hate them!" she exclaimed, her face flushing with sudden passion while her eyes flashed irefully.

"Then it was fortunate he resolved to leave me. You and he would hardly have got on. Perhaps," I said, laughing, "his subtle sagacity pierced the marble of your face when he saw you, and discerned your aversion to his compatriots."

"I thought you were alone?"

"On the first night I was. On the second night I hadn't positively spirit enough to risk a second encounter. But, dearest, I have come to show you over the house."

"I am ready," she exclaimed, her face and manner changing in one of those abrupt alternations that made so curious a feature of her character.

"But first," said I, touching the bell, "there is an imposing ceremony to be gone through. I must introduce you to Mrs. Williams, my housekeeper; a very worthy woman, whom you will find a most useful minister to help you in the government of this little kingdom."

When Mrs. Williams entered I said, "This is my housekeeper, Geraldine;" and then to the other, "Mrs. Williams, this lady, I hope, will shortly come here to take possession of Elmore Court as its mistress. I wished her to become acquainted with you."

She curtseyed without any expression of surprise. Geraldine took her hand.

"I am sure I shall like you, Mrs. Williams. The appearance of this house, so far as I have seen, tells me how valuable you will be to me."

" I am grateful for your kind opinion, ma'am," said Mrs. Williams.

" Are you not surprised to hear of Mr. Thornburn's resolution to marry me?" asked Geraldine, in her pretty downright way.

Mrs. Williams smiled quietly.

" I didn't think it would happen so soon," she replied; " but I guessed it would end in his marrying you, ma'am."

" There, Geraldine," I said, " you see Mrs. Williams knows how I have thought of you."

" Did I want Mrs. Williams to tell me?"

" At all events it is well to have a witness."

She slipped her soft little hand into mine as we left the room; and so, conducted by Mrs. Williams, we passed from one room to another. My darling's delight was genuine. Her child-like pleasure at all she saw was delicious to me to watch. She was

incessant in her praises of Mrs. Williams'
taste and orderliness ; and to do that good
woman justice, she deserved all the admiration she received. She listened complacently
to Geraldine's prattle ; and when she found
that she was no longer required, slipped
quietly away.

We stood at the drawing-room window.
She had thrown aside her hat, and the sunlight made gold of her beautiful hair.

" Do you like Elmore Court?" I asked.

" It is a sweet home."

" And do you think you will be happy
here?"

" Cannot you guess? I feel perfectly
happy now, Arthur ; and that implies great
trust in you—if I did not think you loved
me with all your strength I could not be
happy. Yet there was a time when I
thought I could never be happy again—
never happy again," she repeated, with a

little sigh. "It was winter with me then, but it is summer now. It is sweet to be loved. There are women who say they could live without love ; but I do not believe them. Women were born to be loved."

"Some women were," I answered, toying with her hand.

"I have been very lonely, Arthur. Sometimes I thought I should go mad. It is bad for the mind to feed upon itself. The longer its abstinence the more painful grows its craving ; and to satisfy itself at last, it invents strange fancies and dreadful thoughts —and that is how people become crazy. Your face and voice are a new life to me. I feel that I am not dead now. But there have been times when I thought myself a ghost. Did you ever have that feeling ? It always brought a pain here ;" she touched her forehead. "See there !" she suddenly

exclaimed, " what a beautiful butterfly ! If
I were a little girl I should love to chase it.
But I would not now," she added, shaking
her head ; " those who have suffered much
are always merciful."

" Now, Geraldine, I want to speak to
you of our marriage."

" Yes."   She looked up.

" Are you not a Roman Catholic?"

" I am.   Do you like Roman Catholics?"

" Quite as well as Protestants, though I
am a stanch Protestant."

" After all we are agreed upon the chief
points of religion ?"

" Very nearly.   Toleration is the most
material point in which we differ.   But
Christianity is the religion of love ; and love
is large and can find room for many sects.
But to revert to our wedding—we shall have
to be married in two churches."

" I know."

"Is there a Roman Catholic church here?"

"No. But there is one at Cornpool. I know Father John; he is my confessor."

"How often do you confess?"

"I do not like to say," she replied, timidly; "it is not often enough."

"Once a year?"

"Oh, Arthur, no! Once a month."

"So often?"

"So often! I should confess by right once a week. Would you mind me going to Father John?"

"No."

Let me say this concession was only an act of policy. I determined to try to convert her.

"The want of a church," she continued, "was a great drawback to Cliffegate. But I knew there was one at Cornpool. Yet the little cottage suited me so well, and the place was so secluded, I could not resist taking it."

"Then, Geraldine, we shall have to be married at Cornpool. And now, dearest, when?"

"When you wish, Arthur."

"I want to possess you, dearest. This life is so full of uncertainty that, now you have accepted me, I should not be happy until we are married. Will the end of the month be too soon?"

"Impatient Arthur!" she said, pressing my hand to her cheek.

CHAPTER VII.

WE were married at the end of the month, and when I brought my beautiful bride back to Elmore Court, I thought myself the happiest man in the world. I had reason indeed to think so; for I had marked in Geraldine a depth and earnestness of passion which I felt time would deepen and make still more earnest. And yet what was there about her that forced me into light musings, of which I was hardly conscious of the tenor? Of course, I deemed her love genuine, and I knew afterwards that it was genuine. Yet there was about it a suggestion of oddness, a hint of some sombre presence, which my instincts surely felt, if my heart did not at first recognise.

But her beauty was of the radiant type that sheds a universal lustre on the character. It transfigured her in my eyes. It threw a veil of light over her nature, and hid from my sight those features which a lesser grace must have discovered. My love was apt to give names of its own to the qualities it detected. To me, there seemed no violation of reason in calling her artless, wayward, childlike. I found her capricious conversation fascinating, not perplexing. Her habit of breaking off in her grave speech to chase some irrelevant and simple fancy charmed me. Her composite character suggested the two extremes of womanly sense and childlike innocence, and her beauty filled with light the void that divided them. So that I took no notice of the want of those connecting links, those pauses and gradations of mind, which in reality are as needful to the intellectual character as the middle keys of an instrument are essential to its capacity for producing harmony.

I had proposed that we should spend our honeymoon abroad ; but she would not listen to our leaving Elmore Court. She said it was now in the fulness of its beauty, and where should we find abroad so lovely and quiet an abode? "Did I not tell you, naughty boy, that I would not leave this house?" she had said. "It is the very perfection of a home, in my eyes. We know no one. We can have all the long days to ourselves. I can work in the garden without minding my dress. I should hate to have to keep myself tidy to receive callers— stupid people, who would come to envy and go away to tell stories. Look at my hair now—if I were anywhere else I should have to keep it dressed."

And she pointed at her reflection in the glass, which showed her yellow hair negligently looped behind with a piece of blue ribbon, with stray curls sunning over her white forehead, and streaming down her back.

She seemed, and she was, I am sure, perfectly happy. The gardeners took to her at once; and I would often see one or the other of them following her about to listen to her directions, touching his cap so often as he received her wishes ; and yet, spite of his respectful manner, hinting by his behaviour that he thought her rather more of a child than a woman.

She had wanted to bring her own maid Lucy along with her, but the two servants and Mrs. Williams were enough for our wants. So Lucy returned to the village

with the promise of filling the next vacancy
in Elmore Court.

I purchased a phaeton and a smart little
mare, and would drive Geraldine long ex-
cursions into the country. The memory of
those days is very fresh. She seems to be
at my side while I write, her large luminous
eyes fixed on my face, her small white hand
on my neck, interrupting me with the
musical lilt of her voice to tell me of a
bright-plumed bird that is drinking at the
fountain.

You do not ask me what had become of
the fine resolutions that had brought me to
Cliffegate. You know, for you have doubt-
less experienced, that love is too absorbing a
business to admit of any other occupation.
The living freshness of my wife's society
made my library a kind of mausoleum; and
if I preferred basking in the luxury of her
beauty to handling the dusty skeletons which

lined the shelves, you will not be surprised.
At the time of forming my resolutions I
had never contemplated marrying; and now
that I *had* married, my wife, for the time
being at all events, fully satisfied the craving
for occupation, for something to live for,
which I had hoped ambition might have
appeased.   Yet I did not despair of waking
one morning with a strong impulse to study.
The fact of my life being no longer com-
panionless would disarm the fears of ambition; and I felt that, should I fail in the
attempt to distinguish myself hereafter, disappointment would be qualified, if indeed
not obviated, by the knowledge that I had
always by my side some one to love and
who loved me, and whose happiness it
would be a joyous occupation to minister
to.

Her dislike of society had at first surprised me; but it made me love her the

more. It argued, I thought, her ignorance of her fascination; for I could not doubt, had she known her powers of delighting, that she would never have buried them in so dead a retreat as Cliffegate. She was twenty-seven, a period of a woman's life when her love of pleasure and admiration is strong; though, it must be owned, that this love very often strengthens in proportion as time makes its gratification more difficult. Marrying her as I had, without a deep knowledge of her character, it would not have surprised me had she expressed a desire to change her solitude for a life of pleasure. The dull time she had passed would certainly have justified the wish. Her eagerness therefore to remain hidden from the world pleased me. It illustrated a nature pure and unsophisticated; a heart innocent and sincere. And it made me happy to believe I could always think of

her as my own, without having the calmness
of my devotion sullied by those breezes of
jealousy which society sometimes brings with
it, and which one's particular friends gener-
ally take care shall increase to gales.

We passed our time almost wholly together. She did not like that I should ever
be from her side. She would call me from
a book or a letter, to come and watch her
watering some favourite plants, or any other
work she might be at. And when such an
excuse would be wanting, she would sit by
me, take my hand, and so remain quiet,
rubbing her cheek against my shoulder, and
by her action and eloquent breathing
suggesting the grace and purring of a
kitten.

It was strange that I should have inspired
such a love. This narrative has, I fear,
given you but an imperfect conception of my
character ; yet you may infer enough from

the crude sketch to make you wonder that any one so commonplace as I, should have given such life and movement to the deepest and most latent instincts of this beautiful creature's nature.

She had well said she was born to be loved. Her sensibilities were singularly acute ; her nature warm and sudden ; her sympathies too powerful ; for they agitated her with more joy and grief than the occasion that bred the emotion justified. Her spirit, made tameless by solitude, desired the corrective of love ; her fancies needed sobering ; her longings wanted interpreting ; her whole nature demanded the warmth of imparted passion to give life to slumbering powers, nourishment to sickly instincts, sap and vigour to the drooping qualities which had developed in loneliness and blossomed in sorrow.

Such were the speculations on her cha-

racter I *then* indulged in; and from the
standpoint I occupied they were just. But
when some time had passed, and I got to
penetrate her character more deeply, the
undefinable feeling about her I have before
spoken of became more definite.

I remember well the pain and horror that
accompanied the suspicion when it first
flashed upon me. I endeavoured to reason
the conjecture away; but the very arguments
I brought to bear against it turned traitor
and marshalled themselves on the other side.
I reviewed her conduct; I recalled her
actions, her language, her moods. They
increased my apprehension.

Now that love no longer consented to
blind me, now that I suffered myself to be
possessed with suspicion, I knew that the
truest confirmation of my fear was to be
sought and found in her eyes. The light
that sometimes leaped from their depths,

the vacant dullness that sometimes made them lustreless, were not always the sparkle or the shadow of the mood then on her.

I was alone when I first fell into this train of thinking. She had not left me long; and I heard her singing in the drawing-room as she sought in her portfolio for a sketch which she announced her intention to finish. I threw down the book I held and went to the library. My mood was a strange one : a curiosity and a despair—a feverish wish to know the truth, with a terror of that truth. I strode to and fro, dreading that my face (which I could never force to mask my feelings) would provoke her questioning, and striving to master the miserable doubts that had seized me. But she soon missed me and came to the library, peeping in as was her wont, and then, bounding forward with a movement graceful as a child's.

"You shall not read," said she, taking my hand and pulling me to the door. "I want you to watch me finish my drawing of our home."

"Leave me a little, Geraldine; I will be with you soon."

"Why not now?" she asked, pouting her under lip. And then, coming in front of me, she looked right up in my face.

"Arthur," she whispered, "you look now as you look when you are asleep."

"What kind of look is that, Geraldine?" I said, forcing a smile.

"Come with me and I will tell you."

When we were in the parlour she took a penknife and began to sharpen a pencil. She frowned over her task and then laughed, but so quietly that the sound died in a breath.

"Now, tell me how I look in my sleep."

She laid knife and pencil on the table, and

knelt before me, resting her hands on my knees.

" Did you ever know I watched you in your sleep, Arthur ?"

" No."

" Not by moonlight—though the moon shines bright sometimes ; but never bright enough for me to see you. But when you are sleeping soundly I steal out of bed, and light the candle and watch you. But first I listen to your breathing. If it is calm then I watch ; but if it is disturbed I go to sleep. Shall I tell you why ?"

" Yes."

" Because I never know whether you are dreaming of me or not. If you breathe short and troubled, the expression of your face might give me pain—it would be troubled, too ; and if I were to think at such a time that you were dreaming of me it would make me wretched." She sighed.

"And when I breathe calmly?"

"Then I love to look at you; for you may be dreaming of me. I watch you much longer than you can tell; but I do not look at you too long at a time for fear my eyes should awaken you."

"But what makes you do this?"

"Do I not tell you? Besides," and she averted her face and gave me a sweet shy look, "my watching might make you dream of me."

"But could not I dream of you as well when you are by my side?"

She shook her head. "No. You can make people dream of you by looking at them in their sleep."

"Nonsense, Geraldine," I exclaimed, a little warmly; "this is some crazy old woman's belief: you must not think such things."

I saw her upturned eyes slowly cloud with

tears. Her beauty, too, suddenly took the same intensely plaintive and piteous expression I had marked in her when I had seen her walking in her sleep.

" You are angry with me, Arthur."

" No, dearest," I answered, kissing the tears from her eyes, " I am not angry with you. I only think you should not indulge such foolish fancies."

She smiled. It was like an April sunbeam shining after a shower. Springing from her knees, " Now for my drawing !" she exclaimed. She drew a chair to the table and went to work at once.

Some time after this, in going upstairs I met Mrs. Williams. She stepped aside to let me pass, but I paused on the landing. I had an idea that she was a much shrewder woman than her calm, pleasant, but not highly intelligent countenance would have suggested. I called her to the window on the landing and pointed to the front garden. Geraldine stood at the fountain making a cup of her hands to receive one of the silver threads of water which fell into the brimming basin.

"She seems as happy as a child here, does she not?" I said.

"She is like a child, Sir; innocent and gay as any little girl of five."

"And yet she is very womanly too; and it is this combination of gravity and simplicity that makes her so fascinating. Do you often talk with her, Mrs. Williams?"

"Sometimes, Sir"

"What do you talk about?"

"Oh, of different things."

"I dare say she puzzles your plain understanding?" I said, with a laugh, whose artificiality made it worse than my gravity. "She has a way of breaking off in her speech, of jumping from one idea to

another, that must make her sometimes
difficult for you to understand, eh ?"

She glanced at me and quickly averted
her eyes to the garden.

" Mistress," she said, " doesn't always talk
quite collectedly."

" You have hit it exactly. She is sometimes a little incoherent."

" She is, Sir ; but that comes, I am sure,
from too much good spirits. She's as bright
and brisk as a bird which the eye can't
always follow."

" Do you really think this way of hers
comes from her good spirits?"

" I beg you'll excuse me, Sir," she remarked, folding her hands, " but I should
like to know what you think."

" No, Mrs. Williams, I question you.
Pray be perfectly frank with me. You
must see I have a motive in asking you
these questions. I have faith in your judg-

ment, and I am anxious to hear your opinion of Mrs. Thorburn."

Her fingers worked nervously, and something like an expression of distress entered her face. She remained silent. I looked through the window; Geraldine was gone.

"Mrs. Williams, I am going to ask you a question. The fact of my asking it will convince you of the high opinion I have of your character and how much I appreciate your conduct since you have been in my service. It will imply also the confidence I possess in your truth and secrecy— in your truth to give me an honest downright answer, and in your secrecy to conceal whatever discovery you may make. Do you think my wife sane?"

The answer came reluctantly: "No, Sir."

"What makes you doubt her sanity?"

"Her manners, Sir, and her behaviour,

and sometimes a look she has in her eyes; but her conversation, principally."

"Have you had any experience of mad people?"

"Yes, Sir. Father once took charge of a niece of his that was mad."

"What form did her madness take?"

"She was very cunning. Her mind was full of crazy thoughts; but she seemed to know that if she spoke them she would be thought mad. But she couldn't always hide them. And she was very artful. She would steal things and hide them so that nobody could find them. She was taken worse after she had been with us a year, and we had to send her to an asylum over at Barnstock, where she died raving."

"You would be more likely, after such an experience, to know madness when you saw it than I?"

"Yes, Sir."

"And do you seriously and truly think Mrs. Thorburn mad?"

"You ask me, Sir—it's painful to say— but I would swear there is madness in her."

"When did you make the discovery?"

"I didn't make it suddenly. I had my suspicions after she had been in the house two or three days. But I became sure when, not long after she had been here, she came to me and told me she had seen a shadow in the air of a hand holding a knife."

"She told you this?" I exclaimed, with a start.

"Yes, Sir. She spoke in a whisper, look- ing around her, like one who tells a great secret. Her eyes were all alight, but her cheeks were pale. She told me not to tell you."

"And you kept your promise?" I said,

bitterly. " Why did you not tell me?"
" I hadn't the heart, Sir. I saw how you
loved her—how you loved each other—and
I couldn't speak. Besides, I thought it
might be some wild notion she had brought
away with her from her home. She led a
dull life, and I guessed all sorts of strange
fancies might have taken her in her loneliness. And to speak the truth, Sir, though
I feared that her mind was not right, I
thought your company would bring her
back to herself."

" And do you think she has improved?"

" I am afraid not, Sir."

" What am I to do, Mrs. Williams? how
do you advise me to act?"

Just then I heard my wife singing as she
mounted the stairs, and we broke off our
conversation. I put on a cheerful look;
and when she saw me she came bounding
up, with lighted eyes and outstretched

hands, her face brilliant with a smile. Mrs. Williams had left the landing before Geraldine reached me ; and for my part, I appeared . in the act of descending. She caught my hand and kissed it, a frequent action with her, but she did it with an exquisite grace, as one would do who had learnt her attitudes from nature.

She had a little story to tell me ; how, deep in the shadows of the orchard, she had been watching a green and purple insect crawl from a hole in a tree to a stone, under which it vanished ; and when she turned the stone over with a stick a thousand strange things wriggled away. It taught me something ! it taught me something !" she cried.

I asked her what.

" I said to myself," she answered gravely, " that green and purple insect is a lie, and I who follow it am the world ; for its colours

please me and I can't help pursuing it. And
the stone it has crept under is corruption,
where a thousand other falsehoods, some
pretty and some very ugly, lie hid; and
when I turn it over, I am like a reformer,
who floods corruption with the blaze of
heaven, and all the foul things rush from
the light of truth. Is not that pretty,
Arthur?"

"Yes, dearest; but do you know what
your little fable typifies?"

"What?"

"The Reformation. You were Luther,
the stone was Rome, the wriggling insects
the priests."

"No, no! There never was a Reformation; there was a wicked schism."

"Well, don't let us argue," I said, with
a cheerless laugh.

She had descended the stairs with me, for-
getting the purpose for which she had

mounted them. The harshness of my laugh struck her.

"What is the matter, Arthur?"

"Nothing, darling."

"You do not look as you used. You look frightened."

"Of what should I be frightened?"

"You are; your eyes are scared. Now am I not sharp, to read your face so quickly? Oh, but I know every line in it! I can see the slightest shadow pass over it. It lies quite transparent. It is like the water in the marble basin. I was watching the water not long ago. I saw the tiniest bird, mirrored deep, deep down. Do you know, Arthur, I sometimes think I could fly? I feel so light—so light—I am sure I should only have to put out my arms to rise."

"You would become an angel before your time, Geraldine."

"But I would never fly away from you, Arthur."

"I hope not, for I don't know how I should be able to pursue you."

She laughed. I passed my arm through hers, and we entered the garden.

CHAPTER VIII.

DAY after day I watched her closely.
Fear made observation keen. I had fondly
hoped that both Mrs. Williams and I had
been mistaken—that our commonplace minds
had confounded the brisk and illogical expression of an agile intellect with madness.
But conviction came at last: I could doubt
no longer; her strange speech, her wild
ways, her eyes sometimes startling me with
their brilliancy, sometimes paining me with
their sadness, admitted only of one interpre-
tation.

My pen is powerless to describe the

feeling of misery that took possession of me. The stern necessity of self-control made the suffering more sharp. I dared not by word or look hint my suspicion, lest the avowal, however vague, might precipitate the fruition of her madness. My apprehensions exaggerated the results of observation, and gave to her actions and language a greater importance than they probably deserved.

And all the long days were filled for me with a weird and tearful pathos. For her love grew greater and greater, grew to a wildness and depth that marked her derangement more plainly than any other illustration. She followed me from room to room, into the garden, sometimes at a distance, sometimes at my side. She would throw herself at my feet, rest her cheek on my knee and look up at me with her large and wonderful eyes, of which the beauty became more startling as her insanity grew more vigorous.

I once fancied that her past held some sorrow which might contribute to mature, if it did not actually feed her madness. I had little faith in my power of winning confession; and her exquisite sensibilities and my own clumsy judgment alike prohibited the ordeal of examination. Yet I resolved to question her, and did, at wide intervals, and rather by implication than by direct interrogation; but won no more from her than she had before told me. She said that her married life had been miserable, but that its misery now was forgotten in my love. She never recurred to it. She dared not. She felt that she had been destined for me, and she thought there was something menacing to her future in remembering that another one occupied the position that should have been always mine. The task

of questioning was sadly embarrassed by
her inconsequential language. Day by day
her speech grew more incoherent. Instinct,
so far as her passions were concerned, sup-
plied the place of memory; her memory
grew visibly impaired. She could discuss
with pertinent consistency the first portion
of a topic; but the rest slipped from her,
and she fell with strange abruptness into
another subject, without manifesting the
slightest uneasiness at the sharp departures
of her mind.

I took counsel of Mrs. Williams, who
implored me to conceal my fears from my
wife.

"She is young, Sir," she said, "and her
reason may get the upper hand yet. It is
not as if she was utterly wild. If there's
much strangeness there's likewise much
sense in what she says. This proves she's
capable of reasoning; and there's no telling

at her time of life what nature mayn't do for her."

"My position is terrible," I said. "This kind of existence is life in death. It is hard—it is hard to see one I love so well, who loves me with so pure and rare a love, slowly succumbing to this most awful of human diseases. Cannot I save her? Would a change benefit her, do you think?"

"I doubt it, Sir. It is not always thought wise to change the residences of people so afflicted. Their feelings will reason for them when they are surrounded with familiar things. If you bring them among strangers and into strange places their poor faculties haven't the power to grasp what they hear and see. It's like cutting the thread that supports them."

"But it is impossible that I can sit quietly by and see her decaying, as it were, before me. I must do something."

" Would you like to have a doctor to see her, Sir ?"

" I have thought of that. I have thought of taking her to London. But what excuse could I make—what would she think ?"

" Wouldn't it be better to have a doctor down here, Sir ?"

" To be sure it would," I replied, grasping the idea at once. " I could pretend he was a friend."

" Yes, Sir ; and he wouldn't require to stop longer than two or three days."

" Perhaps not. He would see her in all her moods and come to a conclusion on which he would base his advice."

I was turning from her when she said,

" I believe, Sir, Mr. Martelli is at Cliffegate."

" Martelli ?" I exclaimed, stopping short.

" Why, Sir, so Sarah says," (Sarah was the housemaid). " She was that way yesterday, and says she saw him sitting on the beach."

" I can hardly believe it. What should Martelli do here?—unless, indeed, he has taken a situation at a school—but you have no schools here, have you ?"

" No, Sir. But it is quite likely Sarah was mistaken. She was in a hurry, and the gentleman she saw might well happen to be a stranger. Yet she declares the person she saw was Mr. Martelli."

" Perhaps he has returned to Cliffegate wishing to return to me : but it is out of the question that I could receive him now."

I retreated to the library and wrote a letter to an old medical gentleman who was long my mother's adviser and mine. I set my position before him with the bluntness I knew he relished, and asked him if he could oblige me with the name of any medical man who he thought would have leisure and skill enough to carry out my stratagem. He sent me a long reply, saying he had spoken to a friend who had made the treatment of insanity his study, who would be happy to carry out my wishes. To obviate all chance of exciting my wife's suspicions he advised me to come to London and settle the programme; "for," he continued, "madness is often subtle enough to mislead the most practised observer, and it would therefore be absolutely necessary that Dr. F——'s visit to your house should be so contrived as to seem perfectly consistent with the excuse for his visit which you will contrive."

I saw the wisdom of this and determined to go to London.

As some pretence for my absence was needful, I pretended that I had received a letter on a business matter of great urgency.

A large sum, I said, was at stake, and my presence in town was imperative. Geraldine was very reluctant to let me go. Her large eyes filled, and her beauty became mournful, as though some great sorrow had entered her heart.

" I shall be counting the hours, day and night, until you return," she said. " But how blank the time will be without you ! I shall not care to eat or drink, or go into the garden. Is it not you who make all those flowers beautiful, and this home dear and sweet to me as heaven ?"

" But I will not be long gone, Geraldine. And do you not know that little separations like these sweeten love, as the clouds in the sky make the sunshine more brilliant when their shadows pass ?"

" Our love does not want brightening," she answered, with a sob. " But since you must go, I will pray to the Blessed Virgin to watch over you and bring you safe back to me; for though you do not love her as I do, she loves you and will never forsake you."

I kissed her, and in a few hours after we parted.

I reached London late at night, and next morning drove to the house of my friend. He received me very cordially. I learned to my regret that Dr. F—— had been suddenly summoned to the death-bed of a near relation, and was not likely to return for three days. I thought more of Geraldine than myself. But my friend consoled me by saying that my absence might benefit her; anxiety for my return would give definite occupation to her mind; the longer indeed my absence was protracted the better, for fear and hope would steady by their weight the vibrations of her reason, while expectancy would serve as a leader to her thoughts, marshal them and keep them in a kind of logical order.

I wrote to her, saying that my return was unavoidably delayed, but promised I would do my utmost to be with her on Wednesday. I added that in all probability I should return with a friend, and desired her to tell Mrs. Williams to get the spare room ready.

On the Tuesday afternoon I met Dr. F—— by appointment at the house of my friend. I found him reserved, but gentlemanly. He asked me many questions about my wife, to all which I replied as fully as I could. He announced his willingness to return with me and to give his opinion ; and in reply to my inquiry named a fee which I thought sufficiently moderate.

We left London next morning by an early train and reached Cornpool at about three in the afternoon. I had telegraphed for my phaeton to be in waiting and a little after four we halted at the gate of Elmore Court.

Mrs. Williams received us. I asked anxiously after Geraldine. Dr. F—— drew near to hear the reply.

" I cannot tell what has come over her, Sir. Since yesterday she has been as changed as though she had been suddenly taken with illness. She fretted a little after you left, but she cleared up before long, and got talking with me on the pleasure it gave her to think of your return. I couldn't help taking notice that she talked much more rationally than she used, and I thought that the health of her mind might be coming back to her. But yesterday morning, when she came down to breakfast, I was shocked by her looks. She was white as a sheet; her eyes rolled, and she talked so wildly and quick I couldn't follow her. My fear was that something had happened to you, Sir.

But when I asked her if she had heard bad news from master, she clutched me by the arm and cried out piteously, 'Is there bad news? is there bad news?' I answered, 'Not that I know of.' On which she left me, and stood muttering to herself."

"But where is she now?" I asked.

"She should be in the drawing-room, Sir."

I did not stop to ask if she had expected me; but directing Mrs. Williams to conduct Dr. F—— to his bedroom ran to the drawing-room.

I found her walking to and fro with her hands behind her. Mrs. Williams was right. An extraordinary change had come over her since we parted. Her face was ashen pale; beneath her eyes the flesh had fallen and turned dark; her eyes flashed, but a look of fear came into her face when she saw me.

"Geraldine—dear Geraldine!" I cried, approaching her with outstretched arms.

She stood stock still, then all at once bounded forward with a sharp cry.

"It is my darling boy!" she said, throwing her arms around my neck.

I kissed her; but I felt her tremble in my embrace. I led her to a sofa.

"Did you not expect me, Geraldine?"

"Yes, I knew you would come."

"And you would not receive me at the door?"

"Have you not come to me?"

"Of course I have. But, dearest, you look ill. Has anything happened since we parted?"

"What should happen?" she said, pushing my hair off my forehead. "But I am sick—I am sick for wanting you."

"I could not come before, as I told you. But now that you have me, will you

brighten up? I do not like your worn air.
Those white cheeks do not become you."

" You will give me health, Arthur."

"If God permits me!" I said fervently,
pained by the great pathos of her eyes and
the troubled frightened expression of her
face. "I have brought a friend with me,
Geraldine. Perhaps he will help me to
make you well."

" What friend?"

"Did not I tell you of my intention to
bring a friend from London?"

" Did you?" she asked, with a bewildered
look. Then feeling in her pocket she produced my letter. "How often have I
kissed it!" she said, as though to herself;
" but I do not want it, now that I have him
with me."

" There," said I, opening the letter and
pointing to the passage in it: "do you not
remember reading those lines?"

She knitted her brow like one in deep reflection ; and looking up, with her face softened with rather the shadow of a smile than a smile, answered, "Yes—I ran with it to Mrs. Williams and told her to get the spare room ready."

Just then the door opened and a servant ushered in Dr. F——. I rose and introduced him to Geraldine. He bowed with polite reserve. She inclined her head and sat watching him as a child might.

He appeared to take no notice of her. He began a light conversation with me, wandering from topic to topic, evidently with the design of engaging her attention and inducing her to speak. Now and then I caught him looking at her.

She rose after a little, as if his presence made her uneasy, and went to the window ; but soon returned and resumed her seat by my side. All at once she asked :

"Are you an old friend of my husband?"

"We have known each other some time."

"How came you to meet?"

"We met at the house of a common friend."

"Were you *very* pleased to see him?"

He answered with a smile, "It is always pleasing to meet with one's friends."

"Arthur," she said, turning to me, "it is not fair in you to call anyone 'friend' but me. 'Acquaintance' is what you should call everybody but Geraldine."

"I call you my wife, dearest; and that is a higher name than all."

"Mr. Fenton," she said, addressing him by the name I had introduced him by, "do you think Arthur has any friend who would mourn if he left him for only a day?"

"He is fortunate if he has, Mrs. Thorburn."

"I did, Mr. Fenton. And has he a friend who, if he were lying ill, would wish to be ill too? who, if he were dying would wish to be dying? who, if he were dead, would kill himself, if he could not die for grief, that he might be by his side in the grave?" Her eyes sparkled, her nostrils dilated; she added proudly: "He has only one friend who would wish all this for his dear sake, and she is his wife."

"I am sure he is very sensible of your devotion," he answered, gravely.

She again left my side. So restless was she that even when she was seated her form swayed like one who is ever about to rise. Dr. F—— and I exchanged looks. She abruptly called from the window, "Mr. Fenton, have you seen the garden?"

"Not yet, Mrs. Thorburn," he answered, approaching her.

"Come, Arthur," she called, "we will show Mr. Fenton our flowers."

I wished them to be alone, so I answered that I would change my coat and then join them. Saying which I left the room.

But I was hardly in the hall before she came running after me. She took my hand and kissed it, saying, " Do you think I can be away from you ?"

" But you should not leave our guest alone, Geraldine. I will join you in a few minutes."

" What is our guest compared to you, Arthur ? Have you not been away from me ? It was cruel to bring that man here ; he comes between us ; you are not *all* my own now. He will require your attention, and I shall *hate* him because you give it. I will ask him to go away."

I detained her by the hand, fearing she would actually carry out her threat.

" If you love me, darling," I said, " you will be courteous to this gentleman. You will not refuse me this favour."

"If you asked me to love him, I would try to love him," she answered submissively, her lips tremulous, her eyes downcast.

"That would make me jealous. I only want you to be courteous. Return to him now, show him over the grounds, and justify my great love for you by letting him see how sweet you can be."

She gave me a long look and returned to the drawing-room.

When afterwards I went downstairs I stood at the window watching them before I entered the grounds. They were traversing a broad walk. She looked incessantly towards the house; but sometimes she would loiter with an air of strange *abandon*, or bend to pick a flower and follow her companion with a bound.

Alas! I did not need Dr. F—— to confirm my fears. There was not a look, a remark, even an attitude of hers, that did not now insinuate derangement.

How she loved me! Those earnest glances
at the house were for me. Pitiful it was to
think on such a passion corrupted by madness. What a sorrowful pageant her beauty,
her devotion, her innocence made! It was
the Dance of Death ; the graces marshalled
by a skeleton. Was I worthy of her love?
Yes, for I loved her well, too. She must
have known it, to have been so fond of me.
Instinct in this stood her in the place of
reason. She loved me with her spirit ; she
recognised my love by the faculties of her
spirit. Had her brain interpreted her experiences her devotion must have been less
deep.

CHAPTER IX.

THAT night Dr. F—— and I sat in the
library. Geraldine had retired to rest. Up
to that moment we had found no opportunity for conversation, for she was always
near, always at my side.

I had marked his incessant study of her.
I had admired the skill with which he
directed her attention—as a steersman directs
his bark ; provoking her into speech, perplexing her views to ascertain the consistency
of her mind, then helping her thoughts, to
witness whether her incoherence were due
to normal weakness of intellect or to
disease.

He had lighted a cigar and sat smoking
in silence—a silence I feared to question.
From time to time he looked at me,
with pity rather than embarrassment, and
at last he spoke.

"Mr. Thorburn, I should be in-
truding upon your hospitality were I to
remain over to-morrow."

"I understand. You have no doubt?"

"No doubt."

I mastered an emotion with a struggle.

"Will you give me your opinion?" I
said.

"My opinion is that your wife is
insane. It is impossible that I should pronounce upon the degree of her insanity
from the short time I have been with
her. The conditions with which she is
surrounded must necessarily retard the
growth of her madness. Her love for
you and your presence here exercise a

a restraining influence. Yet I am not satisfied that her mind is free from anxiety."

"What makes you think this?"

"I judge more from her aspect than her manners or language. Her physical condition implies the presence of some active mental pain, which is not due to insanity, though it would aggravate it."

"But what could pain her? She is perfectly happy in my love. She will not suffer me to remove her from this house. Would society benefit her?"

"I think not. If she objects to it she has her reason, and it would distress her."

"Would a change of air, would a change of scene, be of use? I am rich, doctor; do not scruple to prescribe. If my fortune would benefit her, it should be spent."

"I can prescribe only one thing—will you surrender her to my care?"

"No. I could not part with her."

"I am not surprised. Even if I took charge of her, I could not guarantee her recovery."

"I will take charge of her myself. She would never bear being separated from me."

"In one sense," he replied, "you would make a better guardian than I. But the duty of watching the mad is very painful —especially when the insane person is one we love."

"But you do not think she requires watching yet?"

"Not yet. I mean that there is no need of vigilant scrutiny, though I should advise you to keep her well in view. Her madness has not yet emphatically pronounced itself—but it may do so any day.

You must humour her. Her love gives you an influence which no one else could easily possess. I predict, that when her insane moods are most vehement she will prove docile to you." He added, after a pause, "you should procure some woman whom you can trust to watch her. But not yet. Give her perfect freedom now. But when you find it needful to restrain her—and that time I fear will come—appoint some keeper of whose humanity and patience you can have proofs."

"Have you no hope that she will recover?"

"It is impossible for me to pronounce. From the character of the disease in her, I should say it would grow; but its culmination may not be intense. Neither good health nor good spirits will much profit her. Illness, indeed, is sometimes beneficial to madness. I once had a patient under my charge

whom I considered incurable. He was
seized with scarlet fever, which was within
an ace of killing him. He escaped death
by a miracle, and when the delirium
passed, I found he had recovered his
mind."

"But in the case of my wife, should
you think her madness hereditary or ac-
quired?"

"There again you puzzle me. It would
be necessary for me to hear Mrs. Thorburn's history before I could hazard a
conjecture."

"Her history is brief. She married a
man who ill-treated her. Her sufferings
must have been great, for it has made her
detest the world and shun society like a
plague. But I can discern no madness in
this. It would be the natural attitude of
a young mind embittered by wrong.

"As you say, her attitude is no proof

of madness, but the cause that forced her into that attitude may have induced madness."

"You would attribute her derangement to her first husband's ill-treatment?"

" Her ill-treatment may have been one cause. If there were a previous disposition to madness a very painful experience would hardly fail to excite it. In my own mind, I have little doubt that she is oppressed with some recollection, of which the removal would benefit, if it did not cure her."

" Surely, I should be able to ascertain it?"

"Better than any one else. But you will have to be very cautious in your approaches. Yet you will hardly need tuition in such a matter. Your knowledge of her character will teach you better how to act than any suggestions from a stranger. With respect to myself, I do not see that I can be of any further use to you. Indeed, I doubt if my stay here would be advisable. My presence irritates her; and it must be your business to keep her mind as composed and tranquil as possible."

"I am perfectly in your hands, doctor; and however you may act, I am sure it will be for the best."

We remained together until after twelve. Our conversation was entirely restricted to the one subject. He had had much experience of madness and illustrated the information I gave him respecting my wife's derangement by anecdotes of corresponding peculiarities in other cases he had met with. On separating, I conducted him to his room, and then returned to see after the house for the night, as was my custom. At the bottom of the staircase I met Mrs.

Williams, candle in hand, going to bed.

"I am afraid we have kept you up rather late," I said.

"Oh! never mention that, Sir. I only trust and pray that the doctor's visit here may be of use."

"Of no use, I fear," I replied, "except to confirm my sorrow. He does not doubt that she is insane."

"I feared so, I feared so," she said, shaking her head.

"He will leave to-morrow, for he can be of no further service here; and he thinks his presence irritates her."

"He is right, Sir. Mistress came to me this evening, and told me it was as much as she could do to speak civilly to him. 'What does he want in this house?' she said. 'Mr. Thorburn can't be with me as he used before this man came. And he vexes me so, Mrs. Williams. He asks me questions it pains my head to answer; and I don't like his eyes;' and here she began to cry."

"Well, he leaves us in the morning. He is keen-sighted and honourable, and sees that his presence can do no good. I have been troubling myself to guess what could have worked such a change in Mrs. Thorburn during my absence. The alteration is too sudden to be due to illness. Nor is she ill."

"It all came at once, Sir. She was well over night, and next morning, as I told you, I met her looking downright changed."

"Did she not seem suffering at all the night before?"

"No, Sir, I went to bed at about half-past ten, and left her in the library. I thought she might be writing to you."

"Am I to believe," I said, "that a sudden access of insanity would effect such a change? It is possible. Some horror may have seized her in the night. God only knows what dreadful fancies the diseased mind will generate to craze the brain. Dr. F——has told me I must expect her madness to increase, and that it will be necessary to procure some one to watch her. Mrs. Williams, would you undertake such a duty?"

"I would not object, Sir. I would do it from pity. She is so delicate and sweet with all her strangeness, that I could not have the heart to see her in anybody else's charge."

"By doing this you would be bestowing on me an obligation I could not repay. It would almost mitigate my grief to think she was tended by one so worthy and kind as you. Rest assured I shall do my utmost to recompense you for the trying position you will be placed in."

She curtesied.

"I only beg you will keep the secret. I shall continue residing here until I see what form her madness takes. Where else could I secure such privacy—such perfect security from intrusion? From my heart of hearts I humbly pray God to avert from her and me this most terrible calamity. But if it be His will that her madness should strengthen, then we will watch over her as we would over some stricken infant. I may expect tenderness and love for her from you, Mrs. Williams. You will think of my devotion, and will take my place when I am from her side; and cherish, and bear with her; for she deserves it—she deserves it! So young, so beautiful, so fond—to be blighted like this!"

I buried my face in my hands and burst into tears.

"I will do for her, Sir, as if she was my own child," said Mrs. Williams in a tremulous tone, moved by my grief. "She shall never want for love while she is with me."

I took and pressed the kind creature's hand, and passed into the library. The window stood open as I had left it, for the night, though it was the autumn, was close. I entered the balcony. The air was dark; there was no moon; the stars were few and faint. The wind stole through the trees which towered above the house with a hollow plaining.

The gloom and stillness were friendly to thought and melancholy. Away down there among those black shadows I had first met her, walking with a queenly air, her face made marble by sleep, her eyes made sightless by the slumbering of her soul. Into what a life had her beauty led me! The intelligence of my spirit had not deceived me. Had it not inspired me with prophetic forebodings of some such commingling of mine and this fair creature's destinies as was now realised? Of what sin had I been guilty to merit this dread expiation? My love was pure; why was it made a misery?

I was in the act of leaving the balcony when I heard a cry—a human cry, as of some one in pain or distress. It smote my ear—faint but defined; but whence it had come, whether from right or left of me, or from the deep black shadows of the trees beyond, I knew not. I stood straining my hearing to catch the cry again, but it was not repeated.

Was it a human voice? I might have been mistaken. It might have been the dull note of some wakeful bird, humanised by my imagination. It might have been the moan of some homeless dog. I waited wondering.

All at once my thoughts rushed to Geraldine. The cry might have come from her room; its passage through the open window making it sound as though uttered in the garden.

I mounted the stairs gently and opened the bedroom door. A candle burnt on the toilet-table. I glanced at the bed; it was empty, yet her form had pressed it, and the clothes were disordered.

I hastened downstairs, possessed with a strange belief; I entered the balcony, passed down the steps, and gained the garden. I walked forward cautiously, peering to right and left, pausing at intervals to listen, then advancing noiselessly as before. Half-way down the grounds I stopped; I heard the sound of footsteps. In a few minutes a figure in white came out of the gloom and flitted rapidly by me.

I called "Geraldine!" She halted. I went up to her.

"My darling, what are you doing in the garden at this hour? The grass is wet, and you are thinly clad."

"Who are you?" she asked in a hard whisper.

"Your husband—Arthur."

"Let me feel you."

I took her hand and led her to the house. She did not speak until we had gained the library. By the light of the candle I saw that her eyes were dilated, her face quite bloodless, her lips thin, white and rigid.

"Great God, Geraldine! Speak! What is the matter with you?" I cried.

"Let me get to bed—I am weary, weary," she answered.

I closed the window and accompanied her to our bedroom. She moaned like one

under the influence of a narcotic. Her face
was almost deformed by the harshness of
its expression. Her fingers worked incessantly, like those of an infant in a sick
slumber.

" Were you walking in your sleep
Geraldine?" I asked.

She answered with extraordinary quick-
ness, " Yes, I have been walking in my sleep."

" I heard a cry ; did you utter it?"

She laughed quietly, but without the least
change of expression.

" Who else?—who else?" she replied.

" But did you hurt yourself, that you
cried out?"

A shrewd light shone in her eyes as she
answered :

" I stumbled ; the fall awoke me, and in
my fear I cried out."

She began to play with her hair, suddenly
desisted, and asked querulously,

"What makes this room red?"

"It is not red, dearest."

"I say it is!" she exclaimed, irritably. "The flame of the candle is red—the walls are red—your face is red!"

"Your nerves are excited. The shock of awakening has been too great. Lie down, dearest; you will rise refreshed in the morning."

She seated herself on the edge of the bed, looking at her fingers and turning them about. Presently she began to cry, but very quietly. I went to her and kissed her, clasping her in my arms for she trembled as though she were cold. And indeed she was; her hands and cheeks were like ice; but her forehead burned. After a little I succeeded in coaxing her into bed, where she lay sighing as though her heart would break. I watched by her for half an hour, when the regular respiration told me she was asleep.

When she rose next morning she looked very very ill. I was greatly distressed by her appearance and entreated her to remain in bed. But she declared she must get up ; what could she do in bed? She had some work in the garden, and must go to it. I could not help taking notice of her constrained manner, as though she addressed me under compulsion. She appeared to have difficulty in articulating her words; and her eyes, which the sickness of her body seemed to make more brilliant, were restless, startled, and impatient. Before leaving the room she said :

" I do not like your friend, Arthur ; when will he go ?"

" He is going to-day, love."

" Why did he come ?"

Bound to be consistent, I repeated my story of his being a friend whom I had asked to spend a week at Elmore Court, but who

now found he would have to return to
London that day.

" What time will he leave ?"

" In the early part of the afternoon, I
think."

" I do not mean to see him. I'll go into
the garden and hide myself. Do you know,
when he looks at me his eyes give me a pain
in the head ?"

" I am sure he does not wish to pain
you."

" But he does, or he would not look at
me like that. And he asks me questions
which trouble me to reply to. I won't meet
him."

" Very well," I answered, recollecting Dr.
F——'s advice that she should be humoured.

" And do not bring him near me," she
continued, " and do not come and look for
me, for I shall hide myself until he is
gone."

"But you are not strong enough to work in the garden. Why will you not remain indoors? Let Mrs. Williams nurse you a little. You need repose after what happened last night."

"What happened last night?" she cried, looking sharply up.

If the memory of it had passed, I thought it best not to recall it. So I answered:

"I am sure, dearest, you need a little nursing. And should you fatigue yourself in the garden "——

"Tell me of last night," she whispered, creeping close to me.

" Why," I replied, marking her resolution to be answered, "do you not remember finding yourself walking in your sleep?"

She tossed her hands and laughed out.

"Oh, yes, I remember! But go you downstairs and detain your friend while I pass. I will breakfast in the housekeeper's room. Tell him I am ill and cannot be seen."

"Very well," I answered, reluctantly. It did not please me to leave her to herself. Her face looked wax-like, so delicate and transparent was the white of her skin, and her eyes actually trembled with the light in them, as though they reflected the rays of some flickering flame.

I found Dr. F—— in the breakfast-room. I gave him a brief account of what had happened on the previous night, and of her condition. I also acquainted him with the aversion he had inspired her with. He replied that her aversion was an illustration of his influence over insane persons. The first operation of this influence was hate and distrust; but fear soon followed. The motto of the mad doctor, he added, was the expression of the Roman emperor—*oderint dum metuant.*

"She refuses to meet you," I said, "and has gone to hide herself among the trees. You will require no apology for this behaviour," I added, with a mournful smile.

"You do right to let her have her own way. Yet you see how necessary her dislike makes my departure?"

"Yes. It is not wholly impossible that her cunning may have conjectured the truth, and that she has guessed your mission."

"I should hardly think that; though you are right in accrediting insanity with a power of perception which is often far beyond the reach of intellect. The decay of the brain seems to bring the functions of the spirit into activity. But this perception does not always refer to material things. Its proper dominion is the immaterial. Where reason sees order, insanity witnesses disorder; but, on the other hand, insanity riots in the chaos that lies without the limits of normal thought, and delights in constructing theories and forms from the thrice-confounded abstractions it seems to contemplate."

" This would account for many of its delusions."

"After a fashion. But it is hard to reason on the reasonless. The worst form of madness is the total subversion of the intellectual faculties; when the mind represents everything totally opposite to what it is. I remember hearing of two lovers who went mad through a cruel separation. When they were brought together they recognised each other, but each denied the other to be the beloved one. A distinguished mathematician went mad through mistaking the number 6 for an o in all his calculations."

" We can appreciate the horror of madness when it is brought home to us. Much surely may be done by tenderness and sympathy ?"

" They are both severely taxed. I do not utterly despair of your wife, though she will have to be worse before she is better. My parting advice, Mr. Thorburn, is to endeavour to ascertain if she is at all troubled in her mind. If a real sorrow lies there it should be uprooted; if an imaginary woe it must be reasoned away. You must have patience; watch her narrowly; sound her persistently, though with delicacy, and keep her as cheerful as opportunity will allow."

A reference to the time-tables showed a train to be leaving Cornpool at twelve. Having ordered the phaeton to be in readiness, we went for a walk towards the sea. It was his own wish to keep away from the house. The walk was hardly agreeable; my mood was sombre and melancholy, and all my thoughts were with Geraldine. On our return we found the phaeton waiting, and having pressed a cheque into his hand, I bade him farewell.

CHAPTER X.

W HEN Dr. F—— was gone I went in search of Geraldine. I met a servant and asked for Mrs. Thorburn; she answered that her mistress had just come in from the garden and had gone upstairs. I mounted to the bedroom, and found the door locked. I rapped and called to her to admit me. The key was turned, the door opened, and Geraldine stood before me, with the skirt of her dress off, her arms bared to the elbows, and her hair wild. " Come in," she said; and when I was in she locked the door again.

I noticed that her hands and arms were covered with soil; there were fragments of dry leaves in her hair, and on the carpet, from the door to the toilet-table, were marks of her muddy boots. There was a keen look of triumph on her white face; and sharp curves at the extremity of her lips made the expression of her mouth malevolent.

I pretended to take no notice of her appearance. She went to the washstand, brimmed the basin and began to wash.

" My friend is gone," said I; " you will have me now all to yourself."

She looked over her shoulder and nodded.

" I rather fancy he guessed you did not like him," I continued; " for he expressed no surprise at your absence, nor did he desire to bid you good-bye."

" There was a little devil in each of his eyes," she replied; " mocking imps, that made mouths at me and frightened me."

"That is strange. It appeared to me that he had a kind eye."

She splashed the water violently over her arms, and sponged her face, repeating this many times. I waited until her ablutions were ended, and asked, "Where have you been, Geraldine?"

"In the garden, digging, until my arms are tired; and now my head aches."

"But what is there to dig, dear? The beds are in order."

"I wanted exercise, and so I took a spade and dug. I was in a mood for digging. It pleased me to drive the sharp spade into the soft earth and fling it up all quivering. I was in a passion; and I dug a grave for my passion."

"Have you been resting under the trees? There are fragments of leaves in your hair?"

"I don't know how they came there.

Perhaps I dashed the leaves about with my spade. Will you brush my hair out?"

She seated herself before the toilet-glass. How pallid and deadly was the reflection of her face! I loosened her yellow tresses; they flowed over my arm like silk. From time to time I caught sight of her black and glittering eyes watching me; but their lashes veiled them each time I met their gaze.

" I wish I could put a little colour into your marble cheeks, Geraldine. It makes me very sad to see you so pale."

"I would not make my boy sad for much," she answered.

" You were well when I left you; there must be some reason for this change."

" No reason, no reason," she answered, sighing.

" If there is any cause for your illness or for this change, if your heart is oppressed with any trouble or misgiving, if you are not perfectly happy in your mind—why will you not take me into your confidence? Is it not my privilege to share your sorrows? If you are sad and will not tell me the cause of your sadness, must I not fear that you do not think I love you well enough to deserve your confidence?"

"Do I distrust your love? I do not. I am happy in your love."

"If you know how well I love you you must be happy; for no one was ever loved more truly than you."

"Do not talk so, Arthur. Let me feel your love, not hear it."

"Is there anything in the past that grieves you to remember, Geraldine?"

"Hush!" she raised her hand solemnly. "I have buried the past. It will grieve me no more."

"But its ghost may walk," I said, hoping to make myself more intelligible by adopting

her tone. " Tell me how I may find it, that
I may bid it depart and leave you in
peace."

"Should it come, it will not go for you,"
she said, shaking her head. " Ghosts are
deaf, and heed no prayers. They are spirits
and have no fears. The air is full of them
sometimes. I hear their voices, and when
the room is dark I see their shapes. They
are more white than that face," pointing to
her reflection ; " and they have steady un-
winking eyes and long shadowy hands. Do
you never see them ? They often stand at
the foot of the bed and watch us."

" These are foolish fancies, Geraldine.
See, I have brushed your hair well. Will
you do it up ?"

She took the tresses in her hands mechani-
cally and bound them in the fashion she
wore them.

" You do not play the piano as you used,

Geraldine. I have heard that ghosts hate music as much as they hate sunshine or anything else that is cheerful. When you have got on your dress, come down-stairs and play me something, and you shall hear me sing. I had a voice once."

"I do not care to play," she answered wearily.

"You have tired yourself with digging. Lie down a little and I will fetch a book and read you to sleep."

"I could not lie down. How strong the light is! Draw the curtains."

I did as she bade me, and took a chair at the window.

"Do not watch me so, Arthur," she said peevishly. "You have learned that trick from your friend. Your eyes seem as sharp as his."

I averted my face, leaning my cheek on my hand.

" When you dig the earth how the horrible worms crawl out! I cut one into four pieces yesterday, and not one piece was dead when I left. When I die, do not bury me in the ground, but throw me as I am in the sea. The ground is dark and rotting, but the sea is fresh. I can shut my eyes so, and feel myself there. There," pointing in the air, "is a huge black shadow floating over me like a cloud. Great eyes, each with a hundred circles, stare at me through the green water. There goes a great outline, brilliant as a rainbow, white, yellow, black, blue——oh! how horrible it is to die!" she suddenly screamed, clasping her hands and staring at me wildly.

I passed my arm round her neck, kissed her cold cheek, and tried to soothe her. She turned in her chair, burying her face in my breast and trembling from hand to foot. She disengaged herself presently, walked with uncertain steps to the bed, and put on her skirt.

" Is there nothing you can do, my poor wife, to clear your mind of these distressing fancies?" I asked. " If you would try to fix your mind upon something, however un-important, it might create an interest and give you food for thought."

" Are not other people haunted like I am?"

" Many, I dare say.   We all should be, if we did not resolve not to be.   Why, were I to encourage superstitious feelings, I could make myself the most unhappy wretch in the world in less than a week.   Will was given us expressly that we might control our humours, and passions, and weaknesses. You have the will ; you only want the reso-lution to exercise it."

" What can my will do for me?   If I were to grind my teeth and clench my hands, and

declare I *would* not think, could I stop
thinking? Oh! it is enough to drive me
mad!"

She began to talk to herself and moved
about the room, prowling rather than walking; looking uneasily above, then staring at
herself in the glass, shaking her head and
catching at the fingers of her left hand.
Suddenly she stopped, and called out.
"Why will you look at me, Arthur? You
are growing unkind. You used not to look
at me before like that." And she began to
sob.

"It is my love that makes me look at
you; but I will not look if it gives you
pain;" and I turned to the window, and
stared out with as heavy a heart as ever a
man had.

She fell to singing to herself a little
melodious air with Italian words, of which
I caught only the first line;

" Ben veggio che'l mio fin consenti e vuoi,"

and breaking suddenly off, she stole up to
me, threw her arms around my neck, and
whispered :

" Will you be glad when I am dead ?"

" I should wish to die too."

" I wish," she continued, in a half-
chanting dreamy voice, " we could pass
into heaven as we are, without dying.   I
would take your hand, and we would float
to the stars, up through the still air, and on
and on, until we came to the City of God.
There we should be met by the Angel of
Peace, who would lead us to the thrones of
the Blessed Virgin and her dear Son, and in
their holy presence——look !" she cried,
pointing over my shoulder to the garden,
" there is a white form rising—do you see
it ?   I can see the trees through its body—
how steadily it soars ! yet it has no wings.
I follow it.   Look, Arthur."

Hitherto I had not been looking at her as she had desired. Now I turned. Her eyes were wide open, with a fixed stare on the sky; her lips were parted, and she breathed with deep respirations. Presently, she bowed her head, made a gesture with her hand, and crossing herself, muttered, "It is gone."

"Come," said I, taking her hand, "let us go downstairs."

That night, whilst I was pacing the balcony, pondering my position, and less lamenting it than deploring my powerlessness to save my wife from the calamity whose shadow was now on her, it entered my head to search her boxes or trunks for any papers or letters that might throw some light on her past.

Under any other circumstances, I should have dismissed such a resolution from my mind. A wife may have secrets, and her

husband should respect them. But Dr. F——
had intimated his fear that her madness was
being fed by some sorrow. To have discovered, that I might remove, her sorrow,
I would have been guilty of any mean act.
I did not love myself so well as I loved
her.

I pretty well knew I had not been born
with the detective faculty, and apprehended
that my search would be defeated by clumsi-
ness. Still I resolved to attempt it. My
wife had several trunks ranged in my
dressing-room, and one of those large boxes
draped with chintz, called ottomans.

It was midnight before I retired to rest.
I had other things to think of besides this
search. The titles of my books, as they
looked down from the shelves, had preached
a solemn homily on the vanity of human
wishes : and my own experience capped the
moral by presenting me with a picture of

the life I was leading, done in colours as sombre as fancy and reality could supply. When I got upstairs I found Geraldine asleep. I bent over her, and studied her features. The complexion was so white that the outline of her cheek was hardly perceptible upon the pillow. Her beauty had a pinched, worn air. All its calm and freshness were gone; her brow was knitted, her lip curled in a sneer ; she lay quite still, breathing deeply. The general expression of her face was wretchedness. It was pitiful to witness such a look on lineaments so beautiful.

I took the candle with me into the dressing-room, and tried the lids of the boxes. They were open. That of the ottoman only was locked. I sought for her keys in the pockets of some dresses hanging in the wardrobe and found them in a green silk skirt. I turned the ottoman inside out, but found nothing. I applied myself to the trunks, but they were as barren of information as the ottoman. I closed the lid of the last trunk and was about passing from the room, when I heard the sound of a door opened. I listened, then pushed the dressing-room door, and looked out. The bed was empty, the door of the chamber open. I caught a light sound of feet, and stealing to the landing, perceived Geraldine descending the stairs.

I followed her. She gained the hall; I drew near. A lamp that was kept burning all night diffused a sufficient light. I looked at her face, and by the expression saw that she walked in her sleep.

I did not dare arouse her. I had read of the danger of awakening persons from such trances, and Dr. F—— had particularly cautioned me against doing so with my wife. I could do no more than follow her; and this

I resolved to do to preserve her from harm.
She walked steadily to the door leading to the
back grounds, unbolted it, and passed out.
The night air blew chill, for autumn was
advanced and the approach of winter could
be tasted in the night winds. The moon lay
over the trees, slowly brightening, but
shedding little light as yet. But the grounds
and shadows were defined. She seemed
sensible of the chill; for she crossed her
hands upon her bosom and huddled her
shoulders. She was habited only in her
nightgown and her feet were naked. The
dew was heavy ; the gravelled walks sharp ;
yet I dared not wake her.

She passed down the lawn, got on to a
side walk, and marched with slow but steady
step towards the orchard. Soon she entered
it. The shadows were deep, but the moonlight fell through the openings and faintly
illuminated the obscurity. The grass stood

knee deep   My feet crunched the dead
leaves and snapped the rotten twigs.   It was
a portion of the grounds left untouched by
the gardeners at my own request.   The
contrast between the trimmed gardens and
the wild luxuriant orchard pleased me.

Sometimes the shadows and the interven-
ing trunks of the trees made it difficult for
me to follow her.   I wondered whither she
was leading me.   How utterly still was the
place !   Her naked feet made no noise as
she advanced.   Her form flitted and floated
before me in the gloom like a spectre.   She
wound her way in and out among the trees
with precision, while I blundered forward,
sometimes stumbling with my shoulder
against a black trunk, sometimes kicking
and nearly falling over long iron - hard
roots.

Before long she gained the extremity of
the orchard.   The hedge that intersected her

former house from the grounds rose thick
and black. She stood motionless awhile,
then knelt and began to scrape the earth
with her hands, throwing the dried leaves
furiously about her. Presently she desisted,
rose, and went through a pantomime, the
significance of which the gloom forbade me
to interpret; but it appeared to me as though
she struggled with some invisible object.
She breathed heavily and chokingly, and
sometimes faint cries escaped her. Then
down she dropped on her knees again, and
fell to sweeping back the leaves in the same
violent way she had before scattered them.
This done, she left the place, passing me so
close that I had to shrink lest she should
touch me.

She went towards the house fleetly. I had
to walk quickly to keep up with her. At
times she almost ran. As I feared she would
shut the door upon me if I were behind, and

so prevent me from entering, for the other
doors and the windows were bolted and
closed, I ran by her and stood in the passage
until she entered. It happened as I expected. She closed the door at once and
bolted it precisely as she had found it. I
followed her upstairs, saw her get into bed
and lie as motionless as when I had first bent
over her.

I seated myself and watched her. I found
nothing strange in her actions in the orchard.
The mere fact of walking in her sleep was
sufficient to render consistent any extraordinary behaviour. But I dreaded the consequence of her exposure to the night air. I
could not doubt the wonderful providence
that watched over the actions of the somnambulist; but supernatural as might be the
regulation of her conduct, I knew that her
flesh would still be susceptible of ill, and
that there could be no provision made

against the dangers of sickness and disease.

There was to be no sleep for me that night. I felt so wide awake that I saw it would be useless getting to bed. I was agitated and superstitious. The house was so still that I could hear the ticking of the clock in the hall. The wind swept past the windows at intervals and faintly rattled the casements.

How calmly she slept! I could not reconcile her profound slumber with the misery in her face. Was there a sorrow there, or was it her madness that made her face so plaintive? If a sorrow, why should it be undiscoverable? I had searched her boxes; what else remained to be searched? I went to the wardrobe, noiselessly pulled out the drawers and examined them. In the top drawer was her jewel case. It was open. I raised the tray; there was nothing there beyond a few articles of jewelry. I inspected the middle drawer. Here was her desk; a large old-fashioned rosewood box, at which I had once or twice found her writing in the dressing-room. It was locked. I took the keys, fitted the right one, and opened the desk. There were papers here, at all events; bundles of letters, some of them yellow and faded, connected by bits of elastic.

Eager as I was to know the truth *for her sake*, I found my curiosity strongly repelled by my sense of delicacy and honour. Before I could force myself to open the bundle I held, I had to subdue my aversion to the task by recalling the benefit she would derive by my knowing her past. That the rustling of the papers should not disturb her, I re-treated with the desk to the dressing-room, leaving the door ajar, that I might hear if she moved. I then trimmed the light and ad-dressed myself to my necessary but odious task.

The letters were numerous. I read them all. Some of them were addressed to her by her grandmother. Some were written in a foreign hand and signed Luigi. They told me only a portion of her story—that she had married against her grandmother's will and that her husband had been an Italian. The first batch of her grandmother's letters comprised those which had been addressed to her at school. They spoke of her holidays; how glad the writer would be to have her granddaughter with her again. These were full of wise if rather trite counsels. The next batch were those addressed to her at London. These were full of reproaches and threats. There were only five of these letters, and some of them were smudged as with tears. Luigi's letters were addressed to her at school, to Miss Geraldine Dormer, Gore House Academy. They were full of violent protestations of endless love. Some of them began, *Carissima mia*; others, *Bella figlia mia.* One of them contained this passage: "The south is yellow with sunlight, but more splendid is the yellow of your hair. The dark skies of my native land tremble with gems; but more beautiful is the gloom of your eye, which gleams with the light of your soul!" They were mostly written in this strain, diversified here and there with practical questions to which answers were humbly supplicated.

I learnt nothing from them. I returned them to the desk and went to look at Geraldine. She lay perfectly still. I resumed my seat and fell into thought. I wondered whether it was the loss of her husband that had made her crazy. Her marriage with him had been a love match; that was plain from the grandmother's reproaches. Passion, I thought, might easily work disastrous changes in such a nature as hers. But she had told

me her husband had ill-treated her; and her
secluded life, her consistent language on this
subject, confirmed the truth of her assurance.
In my reverie I stretched forth my hand to
toy with a ring that hung from the desk.
Accidentally jerking it, a drawer started out.
I bent forward, and I saw that this drawer contained a flat long MS. volume, together with
a couple of rings, a Catholic medal, and a
silver crucifix.

I extracted the manuscript and opened it.
On the first page was inscribed the word
" Diary." The opening entry was dated
185—.

CHAPTER XI.

The Diary opened thus:

"Here am I in London. I don't know whether to be frightened or glad. Luigi is very kind, but he did not tell me he would bring me to such miserable lodgings as this. Would it not have been better had we never met? I should have known that a teacher cannot be rich. Yet I *do* think him handsome, and he makes love so meltingly that I would rather live in a garret than not have married him. No letter from grandmamma. She is very unkind. Mamma would not have treated me so had she been alive. But

what is an orphan to expect but unkind-
ness?"

A few days later: "To-day I heard from
Miss Cowley" (this was the schoolmistress,
as I knew from reference in the grandmother's
letters). "She says I have acted wickedly and
have forfeited all happiness in this world by
marrying a beggarly Italian teacher. How
my eyes flashed when I read '*beggarly Italian
teacher!*' The cold-hearted thing would
have cried with fear had she seen me. Luigi
is out all day and he comes in tired, and to-
night I thought he received my kiss coldly.
But it must be my fancy. Oh, what a fancy
I have! I think I shall go mad some of
these days."

The chronicle continued much in this
strain through many entries. It recorded
from time to time a letter from her grandmother inclosing five pounds, but repeating
her assurance that she would have nothing

more to do with her. Then the tone of the
diarist grew more querulous; though her
love for her husband deepened, so it seemed,
in proportion as his fell off.

".How can I help being jealous?" she
wrote in one entry; "he is all day long away
from me teaching other girls, any one of
whom he may admire far above me and
secretly love. When I told him this he
seemed to shrink away from my look; and
indeed it was passionate enough ; and he
cried out, half in Italian and half in English,
'God of mine! you will go mad if you do
not keep that devil of a spirit of yours
down!' I threw myself on his neck, and
asked him never, never to cease to love me.
His beautiful eye melted, and he fondled me
with his exquisite grace. So I go to bed
happy."

If her husband earned money she seemed
to benefit little from it; for some of her

records ran, that she had to sit in the dark till he came home, for there was no candle in the house, she had no money to buy one, and the stingy landlady did not offer to lend her a lamp. " To-day I dined on bread-and-cheese and some of the potatoes left from yesterday, fried. If grandmamma knew this she would send me some money. But I'll not write to her about it. No, she shall think I am flourishing ; and if I were dying with hunger I would just wish her to think I had plenty to eat."

Up to a certain entry she continued writing of her husband in warm terms. She avowed her belief that she must be somewhat crazy to find him so fascinating. " Sometimes I think him more so than at other times," she wrote ; but added, " if I am to regain my reason at the sacrifice of my love I would rather be mad." There was a good deal of pungent writing in these entries. I could find nothing to illustrate the slightest mental derangement. But her language was curiously characteristic, and the exhibition of a nature made up of warm and sudden passions, impulsive and generous, but vengeful and arbitrary too, was absolutely complete.

Before long her entries grew somewhat incoherent. She is racked with jealousy. She is certain that her husband has ceased to love her. "I have been married now six months," she says; "how dare I humour such misgivings? But what is it that tells me of Luigi's indifference? Not my bodily eyes, for his behaviour is not altered. The spirit sees farther than the reason. If I loved him with my *mind* I should not have these presentiments; but I love him with my *soul*. It is my soul that is jealous; and the soul is endowed with the vision of immortality and can make the future present.

"To-day is my birthday. I am twenty-

two years old. It has rained steadily since
the morning. I watched the muddy water
in the gutter boiling round the grating near
the lamp-post until I fell asleep. A cheerful
birthday! There was a little piece of boiled
beef for dinner, hard as my shoe, and the
potatoes were not cooked. Yet when Luigi
comes home, he never asks me if I am
hungry. Does he care? He would if he
knew. But how should he know? I
I am always pale, so that he sees
nothing unusual in my white face. I sometimes think he is afraid of me. He said
last night, 'Your eyes flash like a mad-
woman's.' I answered, 'It is with love!'"

There were no records of any hours of
pleasure. Sometimes she chronicled a short
walk. The place of her abode was not
named; but I judged from some references to
the locality that they must have lodged in the
neighbourhood of Leicester Square. The

landlady was a German, and the diarist com-
plained of the atmosphere of the house having
been made all day long nauseating and tepid
with the smell of cooking.

" I asked Luigi before he left for Hammer-
smith to take me away from this dirty house.
But he shrugged his shoulders and said he
was too poor to move. I told him that the bad
smell of the cooking made me sick, and that
the landlady entertained foreigners, who came
tramping in at all hours of the day, jabbering
and singing like savages, and poisoning the
place with the rank fumes of tobacco. ' You
should write to your grandmother to send
you some money,' said he, 'and then we will
seek better apartments.' I told him I would
not write to grandmamma again after her
last letter, no, not if I were dying. ' Then
I am too poor to help you,' he said, stroking
his moustache and humming a tune, with an
air of such cruel indifference that my eyes filled

with tears, though my breast heaved with a passion I could not keep down. 'We have been married a little more than six months,' I said, 'and you are already tired of me.' 'And you of me,' said he. 'It is false!' I cried, in a rage; 'but I suppose you want an excuse for your increasing indifference, and would tell a lie rather than not have one.' 'You did not bring me any money,' he replied, 'and yet you are always grumbling at our poverty. Don't I work like a slave for what I get? 'Tis a pity you are not more educated, for you might go out as a governess, and together we could earn a competence.' 'I did not marry to become a governess,' I said, 'and if you love me as you once professed, you could not name such a scheme.' He made a gesture of impatience, and uttered something in Italian. 'What do say?' I exclaimed. He gave a shrug and left the room. And this is what my dream of love has come to! O how could I moralise if I were not the text! Patience? Yes, I could be patient if I had something solid to hold. But can I be patient holding sand, and watching the grains slipping through my fingers? Oh! my weariness of heart! and my head aches so I can hardly see this paper."

Here there was a leaf torn out. The next entry was dated exactly a year after. The records now became rhapsodical. Strange dreams were chronicled, and conversations which she had held in her sleep.

The first entry spoke of her delight with Elmore cottage. What followed was full of brief references to the past, especially to the events of the year she had omitted to record. Yet brief as they were I could gather the story.

Her husband had deserted her, possibly on the very date of the last entry I have transcribed. By her allusions to her feelings, the shock of his leaving her must have driven her almost mad. " I would thrust him deep, deep into the *hell* he has lighted in my heart against him ; but he comes before me in the night when I am numbed by sleep and am powerless to thrust him off. O what a hate his face drives into me !"

" To-day I came across mamma's emerald ring. It reminded me of that day of hunger when I had to pledge it. I paid the odious German her rent, and went across to the little cook-shop at the corner and bought some cold meat. Do I not remember how delicious it tasted ! How did I live through those days ? I do not know. I sometimes look at my body and wonder how it could have held together under the pressure of so much utter, utter misery. It is bitter to have trusted nobly and to be betrayed remorselessly. It is bitter to feel hunger and poverty and the cruelties of the cold and selfish world. But when these bitternesses are combined, must not the heart be made of steel not to crack and burst?"

How long she remained in this state of destitution I could not gather. But in one entry she recorded her amazement on receiving a letter from her grandmother's solicitor, saying that the old lady had died suddenly, intestate, and that, as the next of kin, she inherited the property. In the same memorandum she referred to the number of names she went over before she hit on one to assume. It was her evident fear that her husband would claim her, should he hear of her whereabouts, now that she had come into property. Under the pseudonym of Mrs. Fraser, and hidden in the obscurity of Cliffegate, she believed herself perfectly secure against detection. This at least is my inference, from one or two passages in the diary; it is probably correct. Some entries before that which I am about to transcribe, the following notice, cut from a newspaper, was gummed:

"March 12, at Courtland Street, London, Luigi Forli, aged 35, of gastric fever."

And beneath it she had written:

"Sent me by Mr. Fells in the letter that enclosed my quarter's money."

Up to a certain point, from this sentence her diary was singularly rhapsodical. Then a more connected narrative began:

"Why did he send me that bouquet? 'Mr. Thorburn's compliments!' He does not know what sort of a woman he sends his compliments to. How I hate compliments! That vile Italian could compliment. Oh! *per Bacco!* his speech was flowery and sugary as a wedding-cake. What came of it? My eyes, my hair, my mouth, my skin, soon surfeited him—though he ransacked heaven and earth for comparisons. If I chose a male friend he should be blunt and sharp—with a hard tongue that could utter words as ringing in their tones as sovereigns. Such a one would not send me flowers.

"Mr. Thorburn called to-day. He must have courage, for he knows my aversion to society. If I walk in my sleep let him thank me; he dared not have come without this excuse. I felt my blood tingling in my forehead and fingers when I looked in and saw that the *gentleman*, as he had announced himself, was a stranger. But the time *rots* so with me—oh! that excellent word just hits the decay of the hours! they drip, drip away, like sodden wood—I could not be displeased at his intrusion. There is life in a new face, and I am beginning to think Lucy too ugly to keep; now that is because she is the only person I see, and her face comes looking in on me through my ugly thoughts and takes their deformity. But he is nice-looking. He is thoroughly English. Oh what a charm there is in a true English face! It is so manly, so genial, so sterling and courageous!—the very opposite to those yellow Italian visages with their red-black eyes and lollipop smirks. I am not sure that I couldn't like this man. He invites confidence, somehow. And there is a big and ponderous ghost called Solitude, that drives me towards him. His eye meets mine fearlessly. He thinks me beautiful. If he were to see me in a passion, with my hair loose and my eyes on fire, would he shrink like my valiant little southerner?

"I rated Mr. Thorburn to-day for watching me. I must like him, to have spoken so smartly. If I could not help meeting a man whom I disliked, I would serve him as my husband served me, and would betray him with such sweetness as would make him think me a witch. I have the power. I think I must be mad at times. Such high thoughts take me that my body will not hold my spirit, and some day I shall see it glide from me and vanish, with just such a laugh as I give when I know I shall not be heard, and when my mood is intoxicating. Let me own here, all to myself, that Mr. Thorburn pleases me. He reminds me of the picture of papa in grandmamma's locket. He must be greatly taken with me to presume as he does. He is too much of a gentleman to force himself upon me as he does if his courtesy did not fall before my beauty. If he should fall in love with me— let him. Am I a celestial intelligence, that I can control a man's heart, and bid it not love, if I choose it should not love? His dream gives him a claim. If I was asleep at the time then must that vision have been my soul which slipped from my body and shone upon him from a cloud. It was possible, and I would have told him this, but his smile can be ironical; and his nature is not yet right for the reception of my beliefs. Why did he kiss the rose I flung away? I can tell; but I will not write it down.

" He was more tender than he was yesterday. His love deepens, and gilds his smile and fires his eye. When I touched his arm it trembled. He makes me no more compliments. He relishes my bluntness, but would he relish it if he knew the sorrow whence it sprang? Sorrow is a rich soil; flowers grow in it sometimes; but more often grow roots that prick, weeds that sting, blossoms whose perfume is poison. Shall I encourage him? If I do, I will not have the heart to say him nay, for he has brought a new light to my heart and a new hope to my life, and my gratitude should make me generous.

"My husband came to me last night. He stood at the foot of the bed. His face was as pale as the dim moon that shone over his shoulder through the window. I thought he had come from the grave, his eyes were so hollow and his hands and cheeks so dry. I clapped my hands and cried, 'Now I thank thee, Oh God! for he is dead, and his shadow has passed from the world.' I awoke. I could not believe it a dream, and crept to the door to see if he stood outside, and went to the window to see if his shadow was on the flowers. All was bare and bleak and white in the eye of that cruel moon, who looks into my brain and chills it with her frosty glare. Then to bed again I went, and fell a dreaming of Mr. Thorburn. How palpable are my dreams!"

The following entry was dated some days later:

"He is making me love him. He has an influence over me, and I find myself listening to his words and cherishing them. He makes me calm. Shall I forego the blessed peace he transfuses through my being? I could love him : but memory will not let me go to him, and like a wrinkled hag casts her long lean arms about me and holds me from him. My heart is empty—there is room for love. My spirit hungers ; shall I not satisfy her cravings? I weary of this solitude. The air about me is peopled with spiritual beings ; I toss my arms, but they will not leave me. They make my loneliness horrible. One in the night told me I should be their queen if I would go with them. But where would they take me? I prayed to the Blessed Virgin for help; but they would not go. Why should they haunt me? I do not invoke them. But if I fix my eyes on any part of the room a shape comes out, and I have to dash my hand to my head and leap like a child to frighten it off."

From this point there was a blank. When she resumed her diary she was at Elmore Court:

"How happy I am! The days go by me like a song. I am loved tenderly and truly; and *my* love grows deeper and deeper, like an onward-running river. But the pain in my head increases, and now and then some of my old horrors return. I stood watching Arthur for an hour last night. He did not stir. His face was calm and happy, and my eyes took their fill of its peace. He does not know I keep this record, and he shall not know. O God! if he knew the past, would not his love fall from him like a garment? But my memory grows weak; and it is well I preserve these jottings, for I could not taste all the sweetness of the present if I had not the past at hand to contrast it with.

"This afternoon I saw a hand that held a knife in the air. I trembled and cowered. It slowly faded and I went on raking. When I met Mrs. Williams I told her what I had seen. The way she looked at me pained me. I saw she did not believe me, though she pretended she did. I do not wish her to think me a liar. I made her promise not to tell Arthur. I would not have him think me untruthful for all the treasures the sea holds."

The character of many entries which followed was akin to this. Some of them contained passages which would appear absurd and incredible in print. Then came this record :

"The room swims and I feel sick—so sick that I wish to die. Arthur went to London this morning, and I cried more bitterly than he will ever know. He cannot guess what agony our separation causes me. It must be a cruel necessity that takes him away. After he was gone, the sunshine drew me into the garden, and I went beyond into the fields, for my flowers give me no pleasure when he is absent. Before long a man came towards me, and I saw it was Luigi Forli. I thought he was a vision, and I tried to waive him away ; but he drew near, and laid his hand on my arm, and turned me into stone. The blood surged up from my heart and made my ears echo with thunder. He talked, but I did not hear him. Then he warmed, and cried out that though I was his wife, he would not take me from Arthur. I said, 'You are dead.' He answered. 'No. I announced my death to get a living.' And he said I must give him money ; he would keep my secret and go away. He named a large sum. He told me he knew I could not give it to him all at once. I might pay it in portions.

He would remain at Cliffegate until it was paid. What was it to him how I should get this money? I had married a rich man, and must get the money under any pretext I could invent. If I failed he would call on Arthur. I turned and looked at him, and he sprang a yard away from me."

A line of writing that followed this was illegible; it broke off suddenly. The pen seemed to have fallen from her hand, for there was a smudge across the sheet. A single entry followed:

" He told me I was mad. I said, 'God be praised, for it gives me courage.' I bade him have no fear. He watched me with glittering eyes; his face was hard with avarice and pale with misgiving. I put my hand in my pocket and said, 'When you receive this you should give me peace.' He shrugged his shoulders, and said: 'I am poor; and since you are my wife and have

money it is fair you should help me to live.'
I pointed to the moon, and whilst he raised
his eyes I stabbed him in the back. He gave
a leap in the air, and I jumped away, for I
thought he meant to spring on me. But he
suddenly fell on his breast with a cry. The
dew fell like blood. I turned him over and
saw he was dead. I took him by the arm
and pulled him under the hedge."

This ended the diary.

CHAPTER XII.

I WENT to the bed-side to watch her.
Her arms lay upon the coverlet; her lips
were apart, and she breathed heavily. Her
cheeks were flushed, and lightly pressing my
hand to her forehead I found that it burned.
I marked now that she slumbered no longer
peacefully. At intervals her form twitched, her
fingers worked convulsively, and once her
breathing was so oppressive that she started,
still slumbering, from her pillow, fighting
for breath.

I could see that she was very ill—very
feverish; and if these twitchings continued

must soon awake.   As I expected, she suddenly opened her eyes and sat upright.   She
looked wildly around the room, and then
stared at me, but without recognition.

"Give me some water," she said.

I filled a tumbler and she drank it eagerly,
sank back, and dropped into a restless sleep
again.   But in a few minutes she once
more started up and asked for water,
adding :

"Give me air.   The bed-clothes suffocate
me.   I am burning."

The fever, indeed, was on her now, and
I knew that she must have taken it from her
exposure in the grounds.   I hastily left the
room, ran upstairs, and knocked at Mrs.
Williams' door.   She answered at once.   I
told her that my wife was taken dangerously
ill, and desired her to come to her at once.
I then hastened back and found that Geraldine had risen from her bed, had thrown the

window wide open, and stood leaning half out of it.

I took her by the arm, and whilst I entreated her to return to bed endeavoured gently to lead her away. She resisted me. Fearful of the consequence of her exposure to the air, I exerted more strength. She struggled violently, and would not stir. At times she turned her head and stared at me with angry eyes, radiant with delirium, but totally void of recognition. Mrs. Williams had now joined me. She at once perceived the danger my wife stood in ; also that she was delirious.

"She must be got to bed, Sir, and kept there," she whispered. "I will help you to carry her."

I indeed needed her help. Frail and delicate as poor Geraldine was, the fever made her powerful as a strong man. She cried and moaned piteously amid her struggles, and

when we had laid her down it took our
united strength to keep her from breaking
from us and rushing again to the window.

She grew exhausted at last and lay still,
muttering wildly and clutching at the bed-
clothes.

"We must send for a doctor, Mrs. Williams," I said. "Is there one in Cliffegate?"

"There is only Mr. Jenkinson the apothe-
cary, Sir," she replied. "But I could rouse
up Hewett" (the lad who attended to the
phaeton), "and it wouldn't take him long
to fetch Dr. Sandwin from Cornpool."

"Do so; and tell him to drive over as fast
as he can."

Geraldine lay back with her eyes wide
open, staring at the ceiling. Her lips
muttered continuously, but the exhaustion
consequent upon her violent struggles
seemed to have left her too weak to articu-
late.

I left her side and paced the room in a mood I must not attempt to define. What was I to think of her diary? That it was an insane chronicle from beginning to end? or that it was true? If insane, how much was she to be pitied! For all that she had recorded as having witnessed, endured and done, must have been more definite and torturing than ever the reality could have proved. If true . . . I dared not think it true. Yet though we may barricade reason with illusion, truth will somehow force an entry. A terror that what she had written *was* the truth, that her final record embodied no imaginary tragedy, weighed upon me like lead. I tried to shake it from my mind.

Mrs. Williams returned. Her presence was grateful. It forced me, so to speak, to break from my hateful thoughts and to abandon for the time being speculation for reality.

The two hours that followed passed slowly.
Mrs. Williams and I spoke across the bed in
whispers. Sometimes Geraldine would start
up and call for water; sometimes would
make violent efforts to leave the bed—efforts
which it took all my strength to resist. As
the time went on she grew worse. She
talked incessantly, a mad wild talk, frag-
mentary as the mutterings of a dream—at
intervals raising her voice to a shriek then
lowering it to a breathless whisper. What
visions passed before those vacant eyes of
hers God only knows! But terrible they
must have been; terrible the scenes they
enacted; for she plunged wildly, as seeking
to disperse them, then wailed entreaties to
them to vanish, whilst her body shook with
strong tremors and the hand which I held
grew wet as though dipped in water.

The morning paled upon the window-
blinds and made the candle-flame sickly.

The birds twittered and distant cocks sang to one another their early defiance. Presently I heard the sound of wheels; Mrs. Williams left the room, and returned some minutes after, ushering in Dr. Sandwin.

He was a short spare man, suave but resolute. He found her calm, for she had worn herself out with her ravings and convulsions. He drew to the bedside, held her wrist, felt her forehead.

" She is in a bad way, Sir," he said. " The fever rages. I will write a prescription, and perhaps you will allow one of your servants to run with it to the chemist at Cliffe gate."

Pen and ink were produced and the servant despatched. He looked at Geraldine curiously for some time and then came round to me.

" There is an expression on the lady's face, Sir, which must be habitual "——

"Her reason is impaired," I replied.

He bowed his head.

"The fever that is on her, Sir, arises, I should say, from a severe chill. I judge that her constitution cannot be strong, and she should have been restrained from exposing herself to the cold."

"She has a habit of walking in her sleep. Last night she left her bed, and traversed the whole length of the grounds on her bare feet and habited only in her nightgown. I feared this result, yet I did not dare awaken her, having been cautioned against doing so. I could only hope that the same Providence that guided her steps would preserve her from any ill effects."

He drew to the bed and examined her face carefully. She lay so still that she looked like a corpse. Her eyes were half closed, and the whites showing through the lids gave her the ghastly aspect of death.

"You look care-worn and anxious, Sir," he said, turning to me; "your vigil has been a long and trying one. Can I induce you to lie down for a little time? Even an hour's sleep would benefit you, and enable you better to meet the demands which your wife's illness may yet make on you."

"What is your opinion of her case?" I asked anxiously.

"I can form no opinion as yet. I shall be better able to do so when she awakens from this stupor. Meanwhile Mrs. Williams" (he evidently knew her) "and I can keep watch."

"I really would try to get a little rest, Sir," said Mrs. Williams. "You look to need it very badly. It is well to keep up your strength, Sir; and I will promise to call you if it should be necessary."

There was wisdom in their advice; I did indeed require sleep. It was not so much my body as my mind that was exhausted. I said I would lie down in the adjoining room, and begged them to arouse me should the slightest alteration appear in her symptoms.

I was chilly. The mornings were cold now, and want of sleep had robbed me of my natural warmth. I rolled myself in a rug, laid myself on the bed, and in a few minutes fell fast asleep.

I was awakened from a deep slumber by some one pulling my arm. The sunshine poured through the blindless windows and filled the room with light. My eyes, heavy with sleep, were dazzled by the glare; afterwards I saw Mrs. Williams. I jumped up at once.

The look of white horror on her face gave me such a shock that I could hardly speak. I heard a whispering going on outside the door. My belief was that Geraldine was dead, and I pressed my hand to my heart while I asked Mrs. Williams to tell me what had happened.

"Oh, Sir," she began, "it is too awful! I—I"——she stopped.

"In the name of God tell me—what is it?" I cried, leaping from the bed.

"The——the——I cannot speak it, Sir; the gardener is below——will you go to him?"

"The gardener! Tell me of my wife; is she dead?"

"No, Sir. But she is raving wildly. She has told the whole story—how she killed him"——she shook with horror.

Something told me what I had to expect. I calmed myself by a supernatural effort.

"Where is the gardener?"

"He is in the hall, Sir."

I left the room. I passed the two servants who stood whispering with pale faces near the door, and ran downstairs. Both gardeners stood in the hall; and both were white as ghosts.

"Now," said I, "what have you to tell me?"

"Oh zur!" said the man called Farley, "I went into t'orchard this morning to git soom apples for cook, and—and I zeed zigns anigh th' hedge of soom 'un having been there i' th' night. The leaves they was all tossed, and—and the ground fresh dug. Zo I went for my spade, thinkin' summut amiss, an' begun to dig to zee what they moight ha' bin oop to. And zur, in diggin' I strook summat zoft, and clearin' away th' mould, coomed across a hand—a man's hand, zur!"

"A man's hand?"

"Oh, zur! I wur too frighted to dig vurther, but throws down my spade, and coom runnin' to th' house to tell yer, zur, of what I'd zeen."

" Come with me, both of you," I said.

" Oh, zur !" they began.

" If it be a dead man, of what should you be afraid ?" I cried fiercely. " Come."

I led the way out, and they followed me. I did not want them to conduct me to the spot ; I knew where it was—I knew where she had led me last night. I entered the orchard, the two men behind me. In a few minutes I had reached the place.

The soil was broken. Around it the dry leaves and grass lay in heaps, as though scattered by a high wind. Amid the newly-dug mould I saw the fingers of a human hand.

" Take that spade and dig," I said.

One of the men took it up reluctantly and began to clear away the mould. Bit by bit, as he dug the moist earth out of the grave, first the arm, and then the body of a man completely dressed, appeared. The

T 2

gardener stooped, took the arm by the
sleeve, and raised the body.

In spite of the soil that obscured the face,
I knew it.   *The dead man was Martelli!*

I gazed upon this awful spectacle with
fascinated eyes ; then my senses forsook me
and I fell to the earth.

For three weeks I lay as one that is dead.
The raging fever that consumed me brought
me to the brink of the grave ; I was snatched
from the jaws of death by a miracle.

When I awoke from my delirium I was
at Elmore Court.   The first object my eyes
opened on was Mrs. Williams.   With consciousness returned memory.   I inquired for
my wife.   The entrance of the doctor saved
her from replying.   He forbade me to
speak, on pain of a relapse.   Nature, utterly
weakened by illness, succumbed to sleep.
My slumber was protracted through twenty-

four hours; and when I awoke I was con-
valescent.

It was then I learnt that my wife was
dead. Her death had occurred three days
after I was taken ill.

Towards the end the delirium had left her.
Reason had regained its power, as though
the soul, animated by the approach of death
and the promise of liberty, had shaken off
the foul hand of madness. She had asked
for me; they told her I was ill. She would
not believe them; she declared that I had
left her. They assured her that I was in
the next room; but she remained incredulous.
A nurse had been summoned to watch her,
while Mrs. Williams tended me. On the
night of her death, the nurse having fallen
asleep, she crept from her bed, stole to my
room, and was found by Mrs. Williams on
her knees by my side, with her arm round
my neck, her cheek against mine, dead.

It was remarked, that after consciousness
and reason had returned, she did not speak
of the crime she had committed, nor did
her conversation indicate the memory of it.
Whence it was concluded that she died not
knowing what, in her madness, she had
done.

When my health was restored, my evidence was taken with respect to Martelli's
death. The inquiry was purely formal.
During my illness the police had vigilantly
investigated the affair, and from Geraldine's
diary and letters, coupled with the testimony
of Mrs. Williams and the inquiries they had
prosecuted into Martelli's career, had estab-
lished the necessary evidence. From those
inquiries I gathered the following par-
ticulars.

Martelli's real name was Forli. He had
been a teacher of Italian at Gore House
Academy, where he had met Geraldine,

whom he eventually induced to elope with him. Her account in her diary of the life she had led with him was in every respect accurate. But you will remember she had omitted the events of a year, and that year was now accounted for. Forli had left her, to live with some abandoned woman, who, after a few months' intimacy, avenged Geraldine by plundering him of his savings and leaving him. It was supposed that he had heard of his wife having inherited her grandmother's property; but his hatred of her, which he never scrupled to confess, coupled with his conviction that had he followed her she would not have hesitated to commence proceedings for divorce, which would have professionally ruined him, effectually served to keep him from her.

I could comprehend his hate, knowing his character, and guessing Geraldine's power of exciting hate in those she hated. When she had found his love decay, when her nature had turned sour under the corrupting sense of his violated vows and her betrayed confidence, I could guess the kind of light his presence would fire her eyes with, the kind of language with which she would lash him into madness.

When he applied again for work he found that his conduct had excited a prejudice, and that the schools in which he had always found a welcome reception closed their doors against him. He resolved to change his name, not knowing how far this prejudice might extend; and the better to commence his life afresh announced his death in the newspapers. He found employment; but his means were narrow, his occupation very limited, when my advertisement met his eye. When he was once with me, it may be supposed he was not very eager to go. He had recognised his wife on meeting her in the fields, but had kept his secret well. When he found that I was resolved to marry her he must have resolved upon that scheme, of threatening her with exposure unless she purchased his silence, which cost him his life.

I suspect he had hardly resolution enough to prosecute his plan at first. He had hung about Cliffegate, so it was ascertained, after he had left Elmore Court, living upon the money I had paid him.

Some years have elapsed since those days. I still occupy the house in London which I took after getting rid of Elmore Court, and Mrs. Williams continues to be my house-keeper. My old dream of senatorial or literary honour has never recurred. Like Imlac, I am now contented to be driven along the stream of life without directing my course to any particular port.

The dead belong to the past, and I will

not ravish from the grave in which she lies that great sorrow of mine which lies buried with her. No record of my grief shall plead for her; no memorial of my despair shall be set down to moderate your judgment of her. She is dead. Her beauty, her love, her madness, are nothing now but a memory and a pang.

LONDON:

Printed by A. Schulze, 13, Poland Street.